Cheryl wiped the █████████████ █ a deep breath. Then ████████████ rst out laughing again █████████████

"What?" He rai ████████████ so funny?"

Cheryl shook her head. "I was just thinking about . . . this. You and me and the slalom course. Annie's convinced there's something going on between you and me, that these driving lessons are just an excuse for us to be alone together."

Steven grinned. "She must not have taken a good look at the VW. It doesn't have much in the way of a backseat."

"Ridiculous, isn't it?"

Steven nodded. "But Annie's not the only one. Jessica was on my case last night, trying to get me to confess that I'm secretly madly in love with you."

"Just because we've been hanging out together, and you happen to be a guy and I happen to be a girl. How absurd."

"It's the way rumors always work," Steven pointed out. "You're guilty until proven innocent."

"Well, I guess it doesn't matter what other people think, as long as we know the truth, right?" Cheryl said lightly.

"Right," Steven confirmed.

They looked at each other in silence for a moment. Cheryl's eyes were warm with amusement . . . and something else. A question? A challenge? Steven felt his body tense with expectation. *Is she wondering what it would be like too?*

SWEET VALLEY High.

ARE WE IN LOVE?

Written by
Kate William

Created by
FRANCINE PASCAL

BANTAM BOOKS
NEW YORK • TORONTO • LONDON • SYDNEY • AUCKLAND

Dara Michelle Kriss

RL 6, age 12 and up

ARE WE IN LOVE?
A Bantam Book / May 1993

Sweet Valley High® is a registered trademark of Francine Pascal

Conceived by Francine Pascal

Produced by Daniel Weiss Associates, Inc.
33 West 17th Street
New York, NY 10011

Cover art by James Mathewuse

ISBN 0-553-29851-8

Published simultaneously in the United States and Canada ·

Bantam Books are published by Bantam Books, a division of Bantam
Doubleday Dell Publishing Group, Inc. Its trademark, consisting of the
words "Bantam Books" and the portrayal of a rooster, is Registered
in U.S. Patent and Trademark Office and in other countries. Marca
Registrada. Bantam Books, 1540 Broadway, New York, New York
10036

PRINTED IN THE UNITED STATES OF AMERICA

OPM   0 9 8 7 6 5 4 3 2 1

One

Cheryl Thomas popped the clutch on Steven Wakefield's stick-shift VW for about the tenth time that afternoon. They both burst out laughing as the yellow car bucked wildly forward, then stalled out in the middle of the Sweet Valley High student parking lot.

"Sorry." Cheryl smiled ruefully at Steven. "I'm probably taking years off your car's life. I'll never get the hang of this."

"Don't worry about the car. It's indestructible." Steven's brown eyes twinkled. "And you *will* get the hang of this—you've made a lot of progress already. I guarantee, one of these days you'll be an excellent driver. So stop being such a typical impatient New Yorker."

Cheryl widened her dark eyes. "A typical impatient New Yorker? No way. I'm a typical laid-back Californian now. I was even thinking of trading in my grand piano for a surfboard!"

1

Steven grinned. "I suppose there's really no such thing as a typical New Yorker or Californian," he amended. "And that's probably a good thing."

"Variety *is* the spice of life," Cheryl agreed. "OK, I'm going to try this one more time. So, I turn the key and then I put the clutch in?"

"Other way around. Put in the clutch and then start the engine." Cheryl did as Steven instructed. "Good," he said. "Now, shift into first gear. Ease up on the clutch and gently step on the gas at the same time. Easy does it. . . . You got it!"

With a little lurch, the VW started forward. Cheryl steered carefully around the parking lot, her confidence soaring as she managed to shift into second gear without mishap. *Maybe this driving business isn't so hard after all!* she thought.

Back in New York City, Cheryl hadn't needed to know how to drive. She and her friends used public transportation: buses, subways, and taxis. In Sweet Valley, though, every sixteen-year-old had a license; passing the driver's test was a cherished coming-of-age ritual.

Soon I'll have my driver's license, Cheryl thought. *I may even get a surfboard, though I'd never give up my piano to get it.* Cheryl had a hunch she would never be a "typical" Californian.

She smiled to herself. She guessed that when people imagined typical California girls, they pictured people like Steven's sixteen-year-old twin sisters. Jessica and Elizabeth Wakefield were blond and blue-eyed, with perfect size-six figures and perfect suntans. Cheryl recalled her first impression of Sweet Valley High. She was pretty sure she had never seen so many good-looking kids gathered in one place—good-looking *white* kids. *Will I be the only black student in the entire school?* she had wondered, feeling incredibly conspicuous.

The student body had turned out to be more diverse than it initially appeared. Still, Cheryl was definitely in the minority, which had not been the case at her school in Manhattan.

"There were so many times during my first few weeks here that I wished I were back in New York," Cheryl mused out loud. "But now . . ."

"Things are looking up, huh?"

Cheryl nodded. "Things *are* looking up, especially at home. Annie and I get along a lot better since her mom's appendix surgery."

"Nothing like an emergency to bring people together," Steven commented.

"It forced us to talk out a lot of our differences," Cheryl agreed. "We may never be as close as Elizabeth and Jessica, but at least we don't hate each other anymore!"

"Liz and Jess are close, but they definitely don't see eye to eye about everything," Steven assured Cheryl.

Cheryl laughed. "Annie and I don't see eye to eye about *anything*. I'll never forget the expression on her face when I told her I liked classical music. She stared at me as if I'd come from another part of the solar system instead of just another part of the country!"

"Even though you're different in a lot of ways, if you communicate, you can be friends."

3

"Yeah. It was a tough lesson, but we learned it."

She pressed in the clutch with her left foot and coasted up to a stop sign. *Steven's such a good listener*, Cheryl thought. *And such a good friend.*

Cheryl had been miserable when her widowed father, a well-known fashion photographer, had announced that they were moving to California. Not only were they leaving New York, but they would be moving in with his fiancée and her six-teen-year-old daughter.

The reality had been even worse than Cheryl's expectation. Suburban southern California was so different! Cheryl missed the big-city noises, the constant hum of activity. Most of all, she missed just being herself. In Sweet Valley, she felt different, self-conscious. She felt that when other people looked at her, they saw a black girl—they didn't see Cheryl Thomas.

Her future stepsister, Annie Whitman, a popular Sweet Valley High student, had tried hard to help Cheryl fit in, but all of her well-intentioned efforts had backfired. First there had been the welcome party, to which Annie had invited just about every minority student from Sweet Valley High, with the misguided hope that Cheryl wouldn't feel so unusual. Cheryl had been mortified. Then Annie had campaigned to get Cheryl into her snobby sorority, Pi Beta Alpha, absolutely the last social organization in Sweet Valley that Cheryl would have wanted to join. When Cheryl turned down the PBA's invitation to pledge, it had been Annie's turn to feel insulted.

Steven was right, Cheryl reflected. She and Annie

4

did a lot better once they finally took time to get to know each other as individuals. Cheryl discovered that Annie was as uncomfortable with this new and unfamiliar situation as she herself was. She hadn't given Annie enough credit; Annie *was* able to look beyond the fact that Cheryl was black. In fact, most of the kids at school were a lot less prejudiced than Cheryl had assumed they would be. She had made real friends, and that made all the difference.

"I think you're ready to leave the parking lot," Steven said to Cheryl. "How about taking us home to Calico Drive?"

The Thomases and Whitmans had bought the Beckwith house, right next door to the Wake-fields. Cheryl took a deep breath. "OK, I'm up for it."

Cheryl signaled for a right turn, then eased up on the clutch and pressed down on the gas. The VW rolled smoothly forward. She was out in traffic. She was driving!

She flashed Steven a triumphant grin.

"Just don't get cocky," he kidded.

Cheryl laughed. Adjusting her sunglasses, she accelerated until she was going at the speed limit. *Sweet Valley's sure a lot prettier than New York*, she thought, admiring the brilliant green of the royal palms and the distant azure sparkle of the Pacific Ocean.

A feeling of contentment, of belonging, washed over her. Yep, things were looking up!

Jessica Wakefield stretched her bare arms over her head with a contented sigh. "I wish it were Friday *every* day."

"You mean Friday *afternoon*," her boyfriend, Sam Woodruff, said.

They were sitting at the edge of the swimming pool in the Wakefields' backyard, their feet dangling in the water. Jessica kicked up a little splash. "Right. Friday the minute school gets out. An eternal weekend!"

"It would always be the very *beginning* of the weekend," Sam elaborated, running a hand through his curly blond hair. "That's the best part."

Elizabeth Wakefield looked up from the picnic table where she was spearing vegetables and chunks of seafood to make kabobs. "But wouldn't that be boring?" she wondered. "I mean, weekends are only special because they come after week*days*. We wouldn't appreciate Friday afternoons if it wasn't for Monday mornings."

Jessica shook her head, amazed at this display of ignorance. Sometimes she couldn't believe Elizabeth was her identical twin, her own flesh and blood. Trust Elizabeth to be unable to imagine a world without Mondays!

"All I'm saying is that this moment is *perfect*." Jessica tossed back her shoulder-length blond hair and extended one slim, bronzed leg. "There are still hours of daylight left, but the sun is a bit lower in the sky, so it's not too hot. The air is warm, the water is cool." *I look great in my new bikini, and Sam thinks so, too,* she could have added. "And there's no school for two whole days!"

Elizabeth laughed. "Well, when you put it that way . . ."

"The fire's ready," Todd Wilkins called from across the patio.

Elizabeth carried the kabobs over to Todd. He placed them one by one on the sizzling grill, then took the empty platter from her hands and set it down on the patio so he could wrap his arms around Elizabeth. "I'm with Jessica and Sam. I kind of like this endless weekend concept," he said, kissing her lightly on the lips.

Elizabeth smiled up at him. "Looks like I'm outnumbered. I'll have to give it a try." She lifted her mouth for another kiss.

They were interrupted by a familiar male voice. "Hey, break it up. Is this what happens when I leave you kids alone without a chaperon?"

Laughing, Elizabeth pushed Todd away. "Better keep your distance," she joked, "or my big brother will beat you up."

"There won't be any violence," Steven promised as he and Cheryl pulled up chairs at the picnic table. "So long as you share your food with us."

"There's plenty," Elizabeth said. "But you're a vegetarian, right, Cheryl? Are shrimp and scallops OK, or should I make some kabobs with just vegetables?"

"Just vegetables would be great," Cheryl replied. "Thanks."

"How'd the driving lesson go?" Jessica asked.

Cheryl smiled. "We made it back here in one piece, so I guess it went all right."

"She's a pro," Steven told the others. "She could pass the test tomorrow."

Cheryl rolled her eyes. "I still stall out at stop

signs if there's the slightest bit of an incline. And I can't parallel park for my life. That's what comes of living in a city where driving is more of a hazard than a convenience!"

"It must have been fun, though, living in New York," Jessica remarked enviously. "Whizzing up and down Fifth Avenue in taxicabs . . ."

"Sorry to disillusion you, but even the taxis weren't all that terrific," Cheryl confided. "I don't miss the city anymore, I really don't. I mean, at first I didn't understand why Mona and Annie couldn't move to New York. But since Dad travels for his work all the time anyway, he was more flexible about relocating. Mona did promise we'd both grow to love it here." Cheryl smiled at Steven. "And she was right."

"Tell us again about how your father met Annie's mom," urged Jessica. "I think it's the most romantic story."

"It was at a fashion shoot," Cheryl related obligingly. "Dad was the photographer and Mona was one of the models. I guess something just clicked between them. He meets a lot of beautiful women, but there was something special about Mona. Which reminds me—they finally set a wedding date, for three weeks from tomorrow."

"That's not much time to make all the arrangements, though," Elizabeth said.

"It'll be pretty simple," Cheryl explained. "Just a small ceremony in the backyard, with lunch afterward. Annie and I are going to be Mona's bridesmaids."

"Will your father and Mrs. Whitman compose their own wedding vows?" Elizabeth asked.

Jessica was more interested in clothes. "What will you wear?" she asked Cheryl.

Meanwhile, Todd pushed back his chair. "I'd better keep an eye on the grill."

Steven was already halfway to the house. "Be right back—I'm changing into my swim trunks."

Splash. Sam cannonballed into the pool.

Elizabeth laughed. "I hate to make a gender stereotype, but I get the impression the males of the species aren't real interested in this particular topic!"

Cheryl smiled. "Tell me about it. My dad wants to marry Mona—he's very enthusiastic about that. But he could care less about all the details. Actually, that makes it fun for Annie and me—we'll get to help a lot."

"That must be wild, helping your own parents plan their wedding," said Jessica.

"A lot of things about this marriage are unusual," Cheryl agreed.

That's the understatement of the century! Jessica thought. There weren't many mixed marriages in Sweet Valley; Mr. Thomas and Mrs. Whitman were breaking new ground.

For a moment, the three girls sat in thoughtful silence. Elizabeth spoke first. "I think it's *great* that your dad and Annie's mom are getting a second chance at true love," she said sincerely.

Cheryl flashed her a grateful smile. "Thanks for the positive attitude, Liz."

"Everyone deserves a second chance at love,"

9

Jessica contributed. "Or a third or fourth. Hey, Cheryl, here's something I bet you didn't know about my dear older brother—he almost tied the knot not too long ago!"

Elizabeth shot a "zip your lips" look at Jessica, but Jessica had Cheryl's full attention now and wasn't about to relinquish it. "Yep, he came *this* close to eloping with his old girlfriend, Cara. She was supposed to move to London with her mother, and she and Steven decided they didn't want to be separated. So they drove to Nevada to get married."

Cheryl's eyes were bright with curiosity. "What happened?"

"They changed their minds at the last minute," Jessica answered sadly. "Too bad. Cara was a really good friend of mine. I wish she were still around."

"Jess, changing their minds was the smartest thing they ever did, and you know it," Elizabeth declared.

"Oh, Liz, you just have no romantic imagination," Jessica complained.

"According to your definition, probably not. And I'm glad."

"Steven's been pretty lonely since then," Jessica went on, ignoring Elizabeth. "I really should be working harder to find someone new for him. And what's *your* story, Cheryl?" she went on. "Did you leave any broken hearts in New York?"

"Plenty of friends, but not a boyfriend, no," said Cheryl. "Well, at least not a *recent* boyfriend."

"Then you're single too. Let's see . . ." Jessica

drummed her fingers on the table. "Who should I fix *you* up with?"

"Not this routine," Elizabeth groaned. "Watch out, Cheryl. My sister's a notoriously disastrous matchmaker."

Jessica put her hands on her hips. "I am not!"

Cheryl's eyes crinkled. "Don't worry about me, guys. Since my piano finally arrived, my life's complete."

Elizabeth laughed. "Just consider yourself warned."

Jessica frowned. "Just consider yourself lucky you don't have a twin sister!"

Two

"I'm so hungry, I could eat a horse," Annie Whitman's boyfriend, Tony Estaban, announced, taking a giant bite out of his bacon double-cheeseburger.

"Watch your language." Annie directed a teasing glance at Cheryl. "There's a vegetarian at the table!"

Cheryl smiled. "Tony can eat whatever he wants. He scored three goals in the first game he's played since he's been back on the team—he earned a bacon *quadruple*-cheeseburger."

Tony reached for his chocolate milkshake. "I missed two other shots, though," he pointed out, as if that somehow diminished the Sweet Valley High soccer team's victory over their Fort Carroll rivals.

After the Saturday-evening game, spectators and players alike had headed for the Dairi Burger, Sweet Valley's most popular teen hangout. Cheryl, Steven,

Annie, and Tony had arrived just in time to grab the last free booth. Now Cheryl glanced around the crowded restaurant. She recognized pretty much everyone there. *This could be lunch period at the Sweet Valley High cafeteria,* she thought, amused.

"I can't believe you're wasting a thought on those missed goals," Annie said to Tony. "You're such a perfectionist."

"Of course I am." Tony slipped an arm around her slender shoulders. "That's why I'm crazy about you."

"Humph," Annie mumbled, but she couldn't keep from smiling. As she looked across the table at Cheryl, her clear green eyes seemed to say, "Thanks." Cheryl was glad to see Annie and Tony so happy. But even though she had done a little mediating, she didn't feel she could take *too* much credit for getting them back together: Annie and Tony made a perfect couple.

"Well, it was a great game," remarked Steven, stealing a french fry from Cheryl's plate. "Offensively and defensively."

"It was so fast-paced," said Cheryl. "A lot more exciting than football, I thought." At her old high school, arts rather than sports had been emphasized. Football might be considered an "all-American" ritual, but it had still been completely foreign to *her.* "I mean, the players aren't buried under pads and helmets. You can see their faces. And their bodies," she added mischievously.

"Wait till track season," said Tony, who was a star distance runner as well as a starting varsity soccer player. "Now, *that's* sport at its purest."

"And the uniforms are even skimpier," Annie promised.

Tony pretended to be offended. "I can't believe this sexist talk!"

"Oh, like the guys on the team never talk about the cheerleaders and how we look in *our* uniforms," Annie shot back.

"Never," swore Tony.

Annie socked him lightly in the arm. "Just for that, I'm tempted not to ask you to be my date for Mom and Walter's wedding. But since you look just as good in a suit and tie as you do in track shorts . . ." Her expression grew serious. "*Would* you come with me to the wedding, Tony? It would mean a lot to me."

Tony bent forward and kissed Annie on the nose. "It's going to be a very special day. I wouldn't miss it."

Cheryl sipped her milkshake. *A date for the wedding . . . you've got to be kidding!* she thought. It hadn't even occurred to her that she would need one. Well, she still had three weeks—maybe she could rustle up a boyfriend by then.

She stifled a giggle. Dating really *was* the furthest thing from her mind these days—she had told Jessica the truth yesterday afternoon. She had met a lot of nice people, but so far there wasn't any one boy she found especially intriguing. *Is it because there just aren't that many black guys in Sweet Valley to choose from?* she wondered.

Then again, Cheryl thought, just because she hadn't landed a boyfriend yet didn't mean she had to be dateless at her dad's wedding. She elbowed

14

Steven. "Hey, what are *you* doing three weeks from today? Would you like to be my escort to the big event?"

"That'd be fun," Steven replied. "I'd be honored."

Cheryl smiled. *What would I do without Steven Wakefield!*

"Hi, everybody. What's happening?"

Cheryl looked up to see Annie's best friend and fellow cheerleader Robin Wilson standing at the end of the booth. With her was Amy Sutton, also a cheerleader and a member of Pi Beta Alpha.

Cheryl gave them a smile. "Hi."

"I'd invite you to join us, but there isn't really room," Annie said.

"Oh, we just stopped by to say hello," Robin told her.

Stopped by to say hello? thought Cheryl. *It's only been half an hour since the cheerleading squad broke up after the game.*

Amy and Robin were looking speculatively at Steven. "So, you're home again, Steven," Robin remarked. "What's the special occasion?"

"No special occasion. I drive down a lot on weekends."

"But not usually *every* weekend," said Amy. "Is college that boring, or is Sweet Valley more interesting than it used to be for some reason?"

Steven looked puzzled. "School's the same, Sweet Valley's the same. What can I say?"

Amy smiled mysteriously. "Nothing, I guess. Well, see you all later!"

The girls strolled off. Steven turned to Cheryl

15

and lifted his shoulders. Before she could comment, Tony's soccer teammates Aaron Dallas and Jeffrey French wandered up to the table.

Steven lifted a hand to high-five them. "Great game, guys."

"Hey, thanks." Aaron flashed a smile. "Hi, Annie, Tony, Cheryl." His friendly eyes lingered on Cheryl in a way she found somewhat disconcerting. Then he spoke to Steven. "So, Wakefield, how come you're hanging out with us small-fry on a Saturday night?"

Steven pointed to his plate. "This place still has the best burgers and shakes in Southern California."

"That's what you drive down every weekend for, a shake?" asked Jeffrey. He slapped Steven on the shoulder, and winked at Cheryl. "Well, enjoy it."

The two boys sauntered off. The subject of soccer came up again and Tony, Annie, and Steven began rehashing some of the game's more memorable plays. Cheryl slumped down in her seat, toying with the straw in her milkshake. *Was that weird, or is it just me?* she wondered.

Glancing after Jeffrey and Aaron, Cheryl intercepted looks from a nearby table. She saw Winston Egbert turn to whisper to his girlfriend, Maria Santelli; Lila Fowler bent close to share something with Jessica.

They're not staring at or talking about me. It's just my imagination, Cheryl lectured herself. Or was it? Her face warmed; she could feel herself blushing. Ducking her head, she pretended to drink her shake. *I hate feeling so self-conscious. I thought I was past this!*

What can people be saying about me? Cheryl wondered. She glanced at Steven's handsome profile. Or was *he* the object of all the interest?

She narrowed her eyes, mulling over the insinuating remarks. "Is college that boring, or is Sweet Valley more interesting than it used to be?" "That's what you drive down every weekend for, a shake?"

People were talking, that much was certain. *But maybe it's not about me, and maybe it's not about Steven, either,* Cheryl guessed. *Maybe it's about the two of us . . . together.*

"It looks like a double date to me," Lila Fowler declared.

"What looks like a double date?" asked Jessica, eyeballing the crowd at the Dairi Burger.

Lila nodded. "That."

Jessica turned to look, as did Sam, Winston, Maria, Sandra Bacon, and Jean West. When she saw who Lila was talking about, Jessica's jaw dropped. "Annie and Tony and Steven and Cheryl? *They* look like a double *date* to you?"

"I know it's radical," Lila drawled. She dipped a french fry in the small puddle of ketchup on her plate. "Defining two girls and two boys sharing burgers and shakes on a Saturday night as a double date."

Jessica shook her head. "Steven and Cheryl are just friends," she said dismissively.

"Sure, they were just friends at *first*," said Lila. "But I think they've moved beyond that. I mean, *look* at them."

17

Once again, all heads at the table swiveled. Jessica studied her brother and Cheryl with a critical eye. They were both slumped back comfortably in the booth. As Jessica watched, Tony said something that made everybody laugh. Then Cheryl said something. As he replied to her, Steven touched her on the shoulder. A few seconds later, Cheryl rested a hand briefly on Steven's arm.

"Wow," breathed Jessica. Lila was right!

"They're eating off each other's plates," Winston pointed out. "That's when I knew Maria liked me—when she started snitching onion rings and french fries without asking."

"You snitched *my* onion rings!" Maria protested.

Jessica was still staring at Steven and Cheryl. At that moment, Cheryl glanced over and caught her eye. Jessica looked away quickly.

"I can't believe I didn't pick up on this sooner," she exclaimed, lowering her voice. "Steven and Cheryl have been falling in love right under my nose and I didn't have a clue!"

"I guess I'm just very good at reading body language and picking up on unconscious signals," Lila said in a superior tone. "My counselor says I'm extraordinarily sensitive."

Winston rolled his eyes.

Jessica really wasn't interested in hearing yet another boring story about the boring counselor who was helping Lila get over the trauma of almost being date-raped. "Steven *has* come home every single weekend since he met Cheryl," she said. The more she thought about it, the more obvious it became. "And all those driving lessons . . ."

"Maybe he's been giving her parking lessons, too," joked Winston. "Up at Miller's Point!"

"I suppose it's natural," reflected Sandy. "From what you've said, Jess, it sounds like Steven's been really lonely since Cara moved away."

"Can't say I blame the guy." Sam crunched into a pickle. "Cheryl's gorgeous."

"And smart," added Maria.

Everyone nodded in agreement—everyone except Lila. "Sure, Cheryl's gorgeous and smart," Lila acknowledged. "But she's also . . ."

Lila didn't finish her sentence. She didn't need to. Jessica was able to fill in the blank, and judging by the expressions on her friends' faces, they could too.

Jessica frowned at Lila. Lila lifted her shoulders in an artless shrug. "Look, all I'm saying is that Steven could have any girl in Sweet Valley," Lila defended herself. "Cheryl's fine for a friend, but I think it's kind of odd that he'd like her *that* way."

"So much for your reputation as Miss Sensitive," Winston said disgustedly.

"Spare me your self-righteous pose," Lila snapped. "You know you're all thinking the same thing, you're just too spineless to admit it."

"*I'm* not thinking the same thing," Jessica declared hotly. "My brother can date whoever he wants!"

"Hey, relax," Sam said in a mild tone. "Don't you think we're jumping the gun here? Last time *I* checked, which was yesterday, Steven and Cheryl *were* just friends. He ate a french fry off her plate—he didn't ask her to the prom. Let's give them a break."

Jessica and Lila glared at each other, but they dropped the topic. Sam and Winston resumed their play-by-play recap of the soccer game; Sandy brought up the subject of who should host the next Pi Beta Alpha meeting.

But Jessica's mind was still on Steven and Cheryl. If she could believe the evidence of her own eyes, and there was no reason not to, then the talk was far from over—it had only just begun.

She looked over at Steven, feeling something like awe. *My big brother is half of the very first interracial couple at Sweet Valley High!*

"See you tomorrow," Steven called after Cheryl as she cut across the lawn to her own house.

Cheryl turned to wave good-bye. " 'Night, Steven."

Pocketing the keys to the VW, Steven headed into the garage. He opened the door and entered the kitchen. To his surprise, his sisters were sitting at the kitchen table, a bag of microwave popcorn between them. "Waiting up for me?" he kidded.

"As a matter of fact, yes." Jessica jumped to her feet and bounced to Steven's side. "So?" she said, managing to load the word with meaning.

Steven blinked at her. "So, what?"

"So, did you have a good time tonight?"

"Yeah. My burger was cooked just right."

Jessica wagged a finger at him. "You *know* I'm not talking about burgers. C'mon, Steve-o, give us the dirt."

Steven looked at Elizabeth. "Help me with this one, Liz."

Elizabeth lifted her hands. "She's got a bee in her bonnet, but I have no idea what it's about."

"I'm talking about you and Cheryl and Annie and Tony!" Jessica explained. "Did you have a good time at Miller's Point?"

Steven snorted. "Yeah, right. Watching Annie and Tony make out is Cheryl's and my idea of a good time!"

"What I'm suggesting," Jessica said knowingly, "is that you and Cheryl might have done more than just *watch*."

Steven raised his eyebrows. "Such as . . . ?"

"Such as, What's going on between you two? Everybody's talking and I don't want to be the last to know!"

Steven burst out laughing. "Me and *Cheryl*? You've got to be kidding."

"The Sweet Valley High rumor mill strikes again," said Elizabeth.

"It's not a rumor if you see it with your own eyes!" Jessica cried.

"And what did you see?" Steven asked. "Me and Cheryl sitting next to each other at the Dairi Burger. Scandalous!"

"It wasn't just tonight," Jessica argued. "You've been driving down from campus every weekend since you met her, and spending all your spare time teaching her how to drive."

"Hardly all my spare time," Steven pointed out. "And what's so strange about my going to a little trouble to spend time with a good friend? Because that's all Cheryl is to me, Jess. Sorry to disappoint you!"

21

Crossing to the table, he grabbed a handful of popcorn. "Good night, girls," he said, grinning at Jessica. He could tell from her pout that she wasn't convinced. Obviously, she would prefer to believe he was hiding a secret romance from her. "Try to talk some sense into her, will you, Liz?" he begged.

He took the stairs two at a time. *What a nutcase,* he thought with a wry smile as he closed the door of his bedroom behind him. Good ol' Jessica and her overactive imagination. Although it sounded like it wasn't just Jessica who was jumping to conclusions.

It always happened that way, Steven reflected as he kicked off his sneakers. If a guy and a girl were good friends, everyone assumed there was something romantic between them. Steven supposed he understood how people could get that impression about him and Cheryl. They *were* hanging out a lot together. In fact, he hadn't spent this much time in Sweet Valley since he was dating Cara.

Steven sat down on the edge of his bed, his forehead furrowed. Cara . . . Cheryl. Now that he thought about it, Cheryl was the first girl he had met since he and Cara broke up that he'd liked this much. She was really something special: bright, fun, attractive. . . . But for some reason, as much as he enjoyed Cheryl's company, he hadn't thought about asking her out. *Why?* Steven wondered. *Because . . .* He forced himself to confront the possibility. *Because she's black?*

That can't be the reason, Steven decided quickly. He didn't think about his friendship with Cheryl in terms of race any more than he thought about race when he was with his white friends. Maybe *indirectly* her race was part of the reason they had become friends; it was part of the reason she had been lonely when she first moved to Sweet Valley, which had led to him wanting to help her get settled and feel welcome. But all in all . . .

Cheryl's being black has nothing to do with the fact that I haven't considered dating her, Steven told himself. There were lots of reasons why he wanted to keep things platonic between them. For example, Cheryl was a couple of years younger than he was . . . then again, Cara had been too. *Well, Cheryl leans on me because she's new in town—I don't want to take advantage of that.* Maybe when a little more time passed, though . . .

Steven flung himself back on the bed and folded his arms beneath his head. Closing his eyes, he pictured Cheryl's face, her smooth brown skin, the twinkle in her big, doelike dark eyes, her quick smile. Without a doubt, she was one of the prettiest girls he had ever met, and one of the most interesting. They found so many things to talk, argue, and laugh about. Black or white, what guy *wouldn't* want to go out with a girl like Cheryl?

Jessica and her friends were the gossip queens of Sweet Valley High. Most of the time they were way off base, completely out of touch with reality. But maybe, Steven mused, maybe Jessica deserved credit for actually hitting on something this time, when she had conjured up a romantic interest between him and Cheryl. Maybe the relationship *was* heading in that direction.

Three

"What a spectacular day," Walter Thomas declared the next morning, pushing aside the sliding glass door that opened onto the deck. "I don't think I've ever seen a sky so blue."

Mona Whitman slipped an arm around his waist. Together they looked out at the lush expanse of emerald lawn dotted with fruit trees and flowering shrubs. "Now aren't you glad we chose Sweet Valley over New York City?" she asked.

Mr. Thomas beamed down at her. They shared a brief kiss. "I think we've made all the right choices, sweetheart."

In the kitchen, Annie was squeezing oranges for fresh juice; Cheryl had her eye on the waffle iron. Now the two girls looked at each other and rolled their eyes.

"My dad isn't always this corny," Cheryl whispered. "I swear."

"Aren't they pathetic?" Annie whispered back. "They remind me of those sappy coffee commercials."

Cheryl laughed. Their parents really *were* on cloud nine these days. It had been a long time since Cheryl had seen her father so happy. *Not since Mom died*, she thought, her laughter fading into a small, bittersweet smile.

She and Annie carried plates, utensils, a pitcher of orange juice, and a platter piled with crisp, steaming waffles out to the deck so they could bask in the warm California sunshine while they ate brunch. *Dad and I might as well be a million miles from Manhattan*, Cheryl reflected. Sometimes she couldn't believe how much their lives had changed in just a few weeks.

They all sat down at the picnic table. Cheryl flipped a waffle onto her plate. "This yard was practically designed for an outdoor wedding."

Mona nodded. "I think we should rent a big white tent. And over there . . ." She pointed to the far corner of the yard. "I picture Walter and me exchanging our wedding vows under a little trellis wound with vines and flowers."

Mr. Thomas reached across the table to squeeze Mrs. Whitman's hand.

"Wow." Annie sighed. "That's so romantic."

"What are you going to wear, Mona?" asked Cheryl.

"Good question. One of these days, we'll have to go shopping."

"I just can't wait!" Annie exclaimed. "I already asked Tony to be my date. Cheryl has a date too."

"Really?" Mrs. Whitman's dark green eyes sparkled with interest. "Who's the lucky guy, Cheryl?"

"Oh, just Steven Wakefield from next door."

"Steven Wakefield," Mrs. Whitman mused. "He's a handsome boy—looks just like his father. He wants to be a lawyer like Ned, too, doesn't he?"

"He's studying prelaw at college," Cheryl confirmed. "Would you pass the syrup, please, Dad?"

"Whoa, no changing the subject," Mona teased. "So, what's the scoop with Steven?"

"There is no scoop," Cheryl said. "We're just friends. I don't know all that many people yet—I couldn't think of anyone else to ask."

Mrs. Whitman turned to her daughter. "OK, what's the *real* scoop?"

Annie smiled mischievously at Cheryl. "They make a *very* cute couple."

Cheryl gaped. "We're not a couple, cute or otherwise!" she protested. "You know it's not like that between me and Steven, Annie."

Annie shook her head, still smiling. "I'm pretty sure I picked up on some sparks between the two of you last night. People are starting to talk."

Cheryl recalled the stares at the Dairi Burger. "Well, they can talk all they want," she said dismissively. "Too bad they don't know what they're talking *about*."

Annie studied Cheryl's face. "I could swear . . . But maybe—" She broke off abruptly.

"Maybe what?" prompted Cheryl.

"This will probably come out wrong." Annie glanced at her mother, then at Mr. Thomas, and finally back to Cheryl. "I don't know. But maybe

26

. . . maybe you just wouldn't be interested in going out with a white guy." Annie blushed slightly. "Sorry to be so blunt. I really don't have a clue about this sort of thing, as you know by now."

"It's OK," Cheryl said. At least Annie was honest. "As a matter of fact, I've never dated a white boy. I mean, it wasn't a conscious choice or anything—I had a lot of white friends in New York. It just happened that way."

"So, something *could* develop between Steven and you," Annie concluded. "You'd be open to it."

"I would and it could, but it won't," Cheryl insisted. "And race doesn't have anything to do with it. It's just that . . ." She stopped short in frustration and confusion. *It's just that . . . what?* "I just can't explain it." She doused her waffle with maple syrup. "Can we just eat breakfast?"

Mona changed the subject, asking Walter about the photo shoot they would be working on together in L.A. the next day. Cheryl focused on her plate. But her mind remained stuck on the topic of Steven, race, and romance.

Their color difference didn't have any impact on their friendship. They never even talked about it— it simply didn't figure in. *Steven's just a person*, Cheryl thought. *It doesn't matter that he's white and not black.* So, in that case . . .

In that case, maybe Annie wasn't so far off base. Cheryl lifted a bite of waffle to her lips, pondering. She liked Steven . . . a lot. What was to stop her from liking him as more than a friend? Didn't the best relationships start out as friendships? Steven was definitely the nicest guy she'd met since she moved to Sweet Valley. He was smart and funny, thoughtful and mature, and *very* handsome—Mona was right about that.

Me and Steven Wakefield . . . It was an intriguing possibility, and all at once Cheryl was very curious. What would it be like to go out with Steven on a *date*? What would it be like to kiss him?

Cheryl's face grew hot. She shot a glance at her future stepsister. *Steven swears that Elizabeth and Jessica sometimes read each other's minds. I sure hope Annie's not reading mine right now!*

"How was that?" Cheryl asked Steven.

Steven glanced out the passenger window of the VW. "Fine, if you don't mind using a gangplank to reach the curb."

Cheryl laughed despite her frustration. "I just can't get any closer."

"Well, I guess I'll allow it," Steven conceded. "You're a mile away from the curb, but you *are* parallel to it."

Cheryl smiled. "Thanks."

Steven looked around the high-school parking lot. On Sunday afternoons, it was deserted. "Enough of this boring stuff," he told Cheryl. "Are you ready to test your reflexes?"

"Sure. Give me a challenge."

"OK." Opening the door, Steven jumped out of the car. He reached behind the seat and pulled some things off the floor: a can of tennis balls, an old sweatshirt, a beach towel, a Frisbee, and a plastic bottle of windshield-wiper fluid.

"What all that for?" Cheryl inquired.

"You'll see."

Steven jogged away from the car. One by one, he dropped the objects on the pavement. When he got back to the car, Cheryl was laughing. "A slalom course!" she guessed.

Steven grinned. He strapped himself back into the passenger seat. "Yep."

"I'll take a shot at it." Shifting into reverse, Cheryl started to edge out of the parking space. "I just hope you're not too attached to that sweatshirt. It may end up with tire tracks across it!"

At a conservative speed, Cheryl looped the car to the left around the Frisbee. Cutting the wheel, she narrowly avoided the crumpled beach towel. "You're cruising," Steven told her. "Piece of cake."

Cheryl stepped on the gas. This time she turned too soon and plowed right over the can of tennis balls. "Darn!" she exclaimed. Struggling to get back on course, she ran over the sweatshirt.

Steven looked over his shoulder in time to see the tennis balls burst from the can and bounce all over the lot. Cheryl braked, bringing the car to a stop. "Sorry," she gasped, helpless with laughter. "But I warned you about the sweatshirt!"

"No problem." Steven's eyes crinkled. "I'll display the tire tracks proudly. I'll tell people I was *wearing* the sweatshirt when it happened!"

Cheryl laughed even harder. "Steven, you're too much."

"That's what everybody tells me."

She wiped the tears from her eyes and took a deep breath. Then she looked at Steven and burst out laughing again.

"What?" He raised his eyebrows. "Now what's so funny?"

Cheryl shook her head. "I was just thinking about . . . this. You and me and the slalom course. Annie's convinced there's something going on between us; that these driving lessons are just an excuse to be alone together."

Steven grinned. "She must not have taken a good look at the VW. It doesn't have much in the way of a backseat."

"Ridiculous, isn't it?"

Steven nodded. "But Annie's not the only one. Jessica was on my case last night, trying to get me to confess that I'm secretly madly in love with you."

"Just because we've been hanging out together, and you happen to be a guy and I happen to be a girl. How absurd."

"It's the way rumors always work," Steven pointed out. "You're guilty until proven innocent."

"Well, I guess it doesn't matter what other people think, as long as we know the truth, right?" Cheryl said lightly.

"Right," Steven confirmed.

They looked at each other in silence for a moment. Cheryl's eyes were warm with amusement . . . and something else. A question? A challenge? Steven felt his body tense with expectation. *Is she wondering what it would be like too?*

Cheryl looked away. The spell—if it was a spell—was broken. "I'm ready for another spin through the slalom course," she announced. "Want matching tire tracks on your beach towel?"

*　*　*

"It feels so good to be riding in the passenger seat," Cheryl remarked an hour later. "Give me a taxi any day."

Steven had taken over the wheel. Now, completely relaxed, Cheryl slumped in her seat and enjoyed the view as they sped north on the tree-lined Valley Coast Highway. She felt good about her driving lesson and she also felt good having talked to Steven about the rumors. He didn't seem too concerned—it was a relief, really, Cheryl decided. Why ruin a perfectly good friendship by getting romantically involved? They'd be crazy even to think about it.

The sun had dropped low in the sky; the pines cast long shadows and the distant mountains were bathed in a rosy glow. Suddenly, Cheryl realized she was famished. "I'm hungry," she said. "Want to stop somewhere for a bite to eat?"

"Yep, and I know just the place. Great burgers for me, vegetarian Mexican food for you, and a fantastic jukebox."

Steven drove another few miles and then turned off the highway onto a narrow road leading up out of the valley into the hills. Soon Cheryl glimpsed a neon sign, glowing in the twilight. "Crooked Canyon Café," she read out loud.

"It's not fancy, but it's fun," said Steven.

He pulled into the gravel lot and parked between a rusty pickup truck and a sleek sports car. "I feel like I've walked onto a movie set," Cheryl told him as they headed toward the café. "Mountains looming in the distance, a huge sky scattered

31

with stars, blinking neon—everything around here is so picturesque."

"Maybe it is a movie set," Steven joked. "We're not *that* far from Hollywood. This could be our lucky night—we could get discovered!"

Laughing, they pushed open the door and entered the restaurant. The place was smoky, noisy, and packed—a young crowd, Cheryl observed.

Steven pointed to a sign. "It says to seat ourselves. C'mon, I see an empty table."

Cheryl stayed close to Steven's heels so as not to get in the way of the bustling waitresses. Country music blared loudly from the jukebox, but suddenly it struck her that the noise level in general had dropped somewhat. *Voices*, Cheryl realized. *There aren't as many voices.*

Her eyes had been on Steven's back; now she looked around her. One by one, as she and Steven made their way through the restaurant, conversations stopped. People stared openly.

A sick feeling exploded in Cheryl's stomach, as if someone had punched her. *It's because I'm black and he's white. People assume we're a couple and they don't like it.*

She wanted to run back to the car, but it was too late. Steven had pulled out a chair for her and was looking down at her expectantly. *Does he notice?* she wondered, sinking into the seat.

Steven sat down across from her. His jaw was set in a tight line and when his eyes met Cheryl's, she saw her own embarrassed, fearful expression mirrored there. He'd noticed, all right.

Gradually, the hum of voices started up again.

Cheryl dared to glance around the restaurant. After their initial curiosity, most of the diners had returned to eating and talking. Only one table of teenage guys with leather jackets and shaved heads still seemed interested. The guys stared openly. One of them made a wisecrack that wasn't quite loud enough for Cheryl and Steven to hear, but it drew leering laughter from his friends.

Cheryl's mouth went dry. She had to clasp her hands to keep them from shaking. The few whispers she had endured when she had first started school at Sweet Valley High were nothing compared to this.

But I can't let it get to me. She sat up straighter, lifting her chin. *I won't let small-minded people make me feel small.* She opened her menu. "What sounds good to you?" she asked Steven brightly.

Steven flipped open his menu, also pretending that nothing was wrong. "The Canyon Burger with grilled new potatoes—I had that the last time I was here, and it was great."

"Hmm." Cheryl considered the vegetarian options. "I think I'll try the chile rellenos."

"Good choice." Steven closed his menu and set it aside. "So, when do you think you'll take your driver's test?"

"Oh, I don't know."

Out of the corner of her eye, Cheryl saw the family from the next table pay their tab and leave. To her dismay, the skinheads grabbed their beer glasses and headed in her and Steven's direction. *Don't sit there,* Cheryl prayed silently.

The punks sat down at the recently vacated table, their stares more insulting than ever. "Um, I—I thought maybe . . ." Cheryl stuttered. "A few more lessons and I . . ."

Steven shot an angry look at the neighboring table. One of the skinheads mumbled something; the others laughed loudly through their cigarette smoke. Steven clenched his fist, but he held on to his self-control. "Next weekend, we'll take out your dad's Buick again," he suggested, his tone calm and even. "After the VW, driving a car with an automatic transmission will seem like a breeze."

It took an extraordinary effort for Cheryl just to nod wordlessly.

The guys were still looking at her and Steven, their stares purposeful, insolent, and unrelenting. Cheryl guessed that the more visibly uncomfortable she became, the more satisfaction they felt—it was fuel to a fire. Her heart beat faster; she blinked back tears of helpless rage. *Is this what life will be like for Dad and Mona?* she wondered. *Stared at, harassed wherever they go, simply because one of them is black and the other's white?* It was so unfair, so wholly and heartbreakingly unfair.

A waitress with a teased beehive of platinum blond hair slouched up to the table. "What'll you have?" she asked bluntly.

Cheryl clutched her menu. "I'd—I'd like the—" Her brain was buzzing with distressed thoughts. Even so, she heard the guys at the next table snicker.

A single tear slid down Cheryl's cheek. Steven's

eyes were intent on her face. At the sight of the tear, he reached across the table and touched her hand. "C'mon, Cheryl," he said in a low, tight voice. "Let's get out of here."

With a grunt, the waitress turned on her heel and stomped off. Cheryl pushed back her chair and stood, energized by the prospect of escape. But first she and Steven had to walk right by the punks with the leather jackets and cigarettes.

As she started forward, Cheryl was determined to keep her cool and her dignity. *They're not chasing me out of here*, she thought. *I won't give them the satisfaction of seeing me run.*

She and Steven were almost to the door when a snide, snarling voice broke the café's sudden silence. "I guess a California suntan isn't good enough for *him*," one of the skinheads observed loudly. "He likes 'em *really* dark."

Cheryl flinched, as if she had been physically struck. She wanted to run out of the restaurant, run high up into the dark, enveloping hills; she also wanted to turn and dash back to the punks, to scratch their eyes out with her fingernails. What could a person *say* to a remark like that? What could a person *do*?

And then Steven's arm was around her shoulders, warm and protective. His strength flowed into her. Together, they walked out into the night.

They got in the car without talking. Steven pointed the VW back the way they had come. He didn't have a destination in mind; he just drove, fast and furious.

I should've hit the guy, he thought, agonizingly aware of Cheryl sitting in the passenger seat with her arms tightly folded. *And I would have, if she hadn't been with me.* But of course, if Cheryl hadn't been with him, if the two of them hadn't gone in to the restaurant together, the incident would never have taken place. . . . *We had such a good time this afternoon,* he recalled, tense and confused. *How did we end up here? Why did this have to happen?*

The car crested a slope. Ahead of them, the Pacific glimmered silver in the moonlight. A few minutes later, Steven coasted into a municipal parking lot bounded by drifting sand dunes. He set the parking brake and killed the engine. Still in silence, he and Cheryl climbed from the car and walked toward the shore.

For along moment they stood side by side, gazing out over the dark, rolling water. Slowly, Steven felt some of his tension and anger begin to dissolve.

He stepped closer to Cheryl. Reaching out, he took her hand and squeezed it tightly. He hoped the touch communicated all the things he wanted to say, but couldn't. *I'm sorry. I'm sorry you had to go through that. I'm sorry I let those jerks hurt you—hurt us. I'm sorry there are people like that in the world.*

Cheryl's fingers twined in his; they held on to each other as if they were drowning. At last, she ended the silence. "That was so awful—" Her voice broke on a sob.

Her pain cut Steven like a knife. The anger flooded back. "What if we *were* a couple?" he demanded, turning to face her. "What difference should it make that I'm white and you're black?"

"It shouldn't make *any* difference." Cheryl's eyes were bright with tears. "I just don't understand it—I don't understand prejudice. Why do some people always look for an excuse to hate other people, to hold them at arm's length, to hurt them? Why can't we all try to care more, to be close, instead of separate?"

"It doesn't make sense," Steven said, his voice low and hoarse.

He put his hands on Cheryl's shoulders and pulled her toward him, wanting to fold her in his arms, to protect and shield her from the cruelty and injustice of the world. Cheryl lifted her face to his—her beautiful, tear-stained face. . . .

Steven bent his head. He put his mouth on Cheryl's and kissed her gently. She wrapped her arms tightly around his waist and the kiss grew deeper, more passionate.

Standing under the stars at the edge of the sea, at the edge of the world, Steven and Cheryl held each other as if they would never let go.

Four

Cheryl closed the front door quietly behind her. She tiptoed past the den, but her caution wasn't really necessary. Walter and Mona were absorbed in a TV movie—and each other.

Annie's the one I have to watch out for, Cheryl thought as she climbed the stairs. She reached her bedroom. Down the hall, rock music pulsed through Annie's closed door; Annie was blasting her favorite new CD. *Good. She probably didn't hear me come in.*

Safe in her room, Cheryl sank onto the bed, her bones suddenly feeling as soft as butter. She was still in the grip of a tumult of conflicting emotions; having to talk to her family right now would be more than she could handle.

What a night! Cheryl pressed her hands to her eyes, thinking back over the last couple of hours. The incident at the Crooked Canyon Café stood out in her mind all too clearly. It had been horrible, but she could comprehend it—she knew what those skinheads were about. But what had taken place between her and Steven at the beach ... what exactly was *that* about?

A knock on her door jolted Cheryl from her reverie. "Who is it?"

Annie eased open the door. "Hi, it's just me."

"Hi."

Cheryl hoped her flat tone communicated that she wasn't in the mood for a sisterly chat. No such luck. Annie made herself comfortable on the bed alongside Cheryl. "You guys were out pretty late," she observed with a teasing smile. "Were you practicing your night driving?"

Cheryl didn't respond. Annie's eyes searched her face. "Cheryl, is something wrong? What happened?" She put a hand on Cheryl's arm. "Cheryl, you're shaking! Did you have an accident?"

Cheryl shook her head. "No, we didn't have ... an accident." She searched her memory for a good place to start. But where did this particular story begin? "We ended up at the beach," Cheryl said at last. "Steven ... kissed me."

Annie's eyes grew as wide as saucers. "*And?*" she pressed.

Annie's curiosity was so open, so childlike, Cheryl couldn't help smiling. "And ... I kissed him back. I guess our relationship has shifted gears," she added dryly. "No pun intended."

"Oh, Cheryl!" Annie flung her arms around Cheryl. "Congratulations. I'm so happy for you two!"

Cheryl patted Annie's back awkwardly. "Um, thanks, Annie."

"I'd been thinking that a boyfriend was just what you needed to make you feel more at home in Sweet Valley," Annie rattled on. "And Steven Wakefield is just the greatest guy. This is perfect!"

Perfect? Cheryl couldn't help remembering Annie's remark at brunch that morning, about Steven being white. She hadn't brought it up again, but it had to be on her mind. It would be on *everybody's* mind once word got around, Cheryl suspected. Maybe people in Sweet Valley wouldn't react like the punks at the Crooked Canyon Café, but the judgment, the condemnation, were bound to be there . . . under the surface.

"I don't care what people think," Cheryl declared defiantly. She pulled away from Annie. "An interracial romance is OK for Dad and Mona, and it's OK for Steven and me."

Annie's slender eyebrows shot up. "Well, sure. Of course it's OK. Everyone'll be fine about it—I wouldn't worry."

"Everyone *won't* be fine," Cheryl argued. "Kids at school are going to talk about me more than ever."

Annie shook her head, her dark hair swinging against her face. "People will be happy for you, just like I am," she insisted.

"We'll see," Cheryl predicted, her tone making it clear that she didn't expect to see anything good. *Annie should have been there*, she thought. *She should've felt those stares, listened to those insults. . . .* Cheryl clenched her fists. No one could persuade her that she and Steven weren't going against the odds. The question was, could they *beat* the odds?

"Steven's still home," Elizabeth remarked on Monday afternoon, nodding toward his car as she set the parking brake on the Jeep.

Jessica climbed out, dragging her book bag after her. "That's right. He had a three-day weekend, the lucky bum."

"Did you see him at all last night?" Elizabeth asked. "I don't remember hearing him come in, but then I was pretty busy finishing that article for *The Oracle*."

Jessica shook her head. "I was studying over at Sam's, remember?"

Elizabeth grinned. "Yeah, and I bet you got a lot of work done."

Jessica smiled, her dimple deepening. "I learned a number of new things . . . about Sam. He has the *cutest* freckle—guess where?"

"I don't want to know!"

As usual, the twins headed straight into the kitchen, in search of an afternoon snack. They found their brother in shorts and a rumpled T-shirt, sitting at the counter with a cup of coffee.

"*Don't* tell me you just woke up," Jessica said indignantly. "Rub it in, why don't you."

"I had a hard time falling asleep last night. I must've been awake until four or five in the morning, tossing and turning," he explained. "So I slept in."

Elizabeth opened the fridge and pulled out a bottle of grapefruit juice. "Since when are you an insomniac?" she asked.

41

"I guess I just had a lot on my mind."

"Such as?" Jessica prompted, tearing open a box of gingersnaps.

"Such as . . . Cheryl." A half smile touched Steven's face. "I might as well tell you. You'll find out sooner or later."

"Tell us what?" Jessica squealed.

"Well, last night, Cheryl and I . . . We went for a walk on the beach, and I guess you could say we're now . . . romantically involved."

"Steven! That's fantastic!" Jessica whirled to face her twin, her expression triumphant. "I knew it! Didn't I tell you, Liz?"

Elizabeth smiled. "What can I say, Jess? You're omniscient." Crossing to Steven's side, she dropped a kiss on her brother's cheek. "This is great news, Steven."

Steven studied her face closely. "Do you really think so?" he challenged her.

"Of course," Elizabeth said, surprised. "I'm happy for you."

Steven sipped his coffee. "You're not just saying that, are you? Because there's nothing that bugs me more than people who say one thing and think another. I mean, I'd understand if you felt a little bit . . . shocked. You can admit it."

Now Jessica and Elizabeth both were staring at Steven. Jessica wrinkled her nose, puzzled. "Shocked? You mean, just because she's—"

"A lot of people are going to give me and Cheryl a hard time about this," Steven broke in. "We're going to face a lot of opposition."

"But not from us!" Elizabeth exclaimed, hurt that

42

Steven would expect a negative response from his own sisters. "Give us a little credit."

"Yeah," Jessica chimed in. "We like Cheryl, and we *love* you."

"Sorry," Steven said, still sounding defensive. "But the fact is, people are going to talk. Cheryl and I will just have to rise above it, and it'll be an uphill battle."

Elizabeth nodded. She didn't reply; she didn't know how to. It seemed no matter what she said, Steven was determined to take it the wrong way.

"Hey, I heard about a great secondhand car someone at school is selling," Jessica told Steven, offering him a gingersnap. "It'd be perfect for Cheryl once she gets her license."

Elizabeth listened as her brother and sister gabbed, a tiny frown creasing her forehead. Steven's announcement left her with an odd feeling. *He's not exactly starry-eyed*, she reflected. He wasn't acting like a guy in love. He was acting like he was out to prove something. *But what?* Elizabeth wondered. *And to whom?*

Steven said people were going to talk, Jessica mused. *And boy, was he right!*

As usual, the latest gossip had swept through the halls of Sweet Valley High at warp speed. Jessica imagined everybody knew by now—and it was only lunchtime on Tuesday.

As she and Amy headed down the crowded hall toward the cafeteria, Jessica overheard yet another opinion about her brother and Cheryl's new relationship. Two sophomore girls had their heads so close together, they didn't notice Jessica, who was practically stepping on their heels.

". . . Elizabeth and Jessica's older brother, Steven," one girl was saying in a loud whisper. "He went out with Cara Walker before she moved to England, remember? And now supposedly he's dating Cheryl Thomas!"

"It sure didn't take Cheryl long to land a guy," the other girl observed. "You'd think she would've picked someone . . ."

The girl left her sentence unfinished, but her meaning came across loud and clear. *Why don't you spit it out?* Jessica felt like yelling at her. *Don't pretend to be ladylike and tactful when really you're a narrow-minded wimp!*

"I know what you mean," the first girl responded. "I just can't see it, from Cheryl's point of view *or* from Steven's. I for one could *never* be attracted to—"

Jessica had heard enough. Clearing her throat loudly, she elbowed past the two girls, glaring at them as she did so that she could watch, with profound satisfaction, as their faces turned scarlet.

"Could you believe that?" she fumed at Amy as they joined the lunch line in the cafeteria. "What a couple of brainless idiots!"

"They were total airheads," Amy agreed, reaching for a plastic-wrapped chicken-salad sandwich. "But they probably didn't mean to sound malicious. A lot of people just don't know what to think or say about this interracial-romance stuff. It caught a lot of us by surprise."

Jessica grabbed a carton of yogurt and a bran muffin and tossed them on her tray. "Well, on Steven's behalf, I'm outraged," she declared. "*And* on Cheryl's," she added as an afterthought.

Jessica and Amy paid for their lunches, then scanned the packed cafeteria for a table. "Guess what the topic of conversation is going to be?" Amy ribbed Jessica as they made their way to where Lila was sitting with Maria, Winston, Jean, Scott Frost, Suzanne Hanlon, and Caroline Pearce.

Sure enough, all seven voices were buzzing excitedly. The chatter stopped abruptly when Jessica appeared.

"Don't let me spoil the fun," Jessica said sarcastically, pulling out the empty chair next to Scott.

Jean leaned in front of her boyfriend in order to gaze with exaggerated sincerity into Jessica's eyes. "I just want to be the first to tell you that I think it's *wonderful* that Steven and Cheryl are dating," she gushed. "They make a very glamorous couple."

"Why, thank you, Jeanie," Jessica said loftily.

Winston snorted. "I really don't get why everyone has to make such an issue out of this. Boy meets girl, they fall in love, big deal! There wasn't an uproar like this when Maria and I started going out."

"Oh, yes, there was," Lila drawled. "No one could *believe* a halfway intelligent girl like Maria would actually go out with a clown like you, remember?"

Maria gave Lila a dirty look. "It *is* more complicated than that," she said to Winston. "Let's face it, Steven and Cheryl are a first."

"They're pioneers, trailblazers," Scott said with enthusiasm.

Jessica liked the sound of that. "My brother has courage and conviction," she declared. "He's not about to let other people's hang-ups influence him. Don't you ever go to the movies? True romance recognizes no barriers."

Lila rolled her eyes. "True romance. Give me a break."

Suzanne had also listened to this exchange with thinly disguised skepticism. Now she pursed her lips. "I suppose Steven's old enough to know what he's doing. I can't help thinking, though, that he'd be *happier* dating someone more like . . . Cara, for example. And wouldn't Cheryl be more comfortable going out with a guy who shared her background?"

"You mean her skin color, don't you?" Maria asked dryly.

Caroline leaned forward, her elbows on the table. "I don't get it, either," she confessed. "If you ask me, Steven and Cheryl are making a big mistake. They're just asking for trouble. They'll never fit in."

"They're not asking for trouble!" Jessica's eyes flashed with indignation. "They're not asking for anything but tolerance."

"Unfortunately, it looks like that's in short supply," observed Winston.

"Are you sure you girls aren't just still miffed because Cheryl didn't want to join PBA?" Scott asked Lila, Suzanne, and Caroline.

"Scott!" Jean elbowed her boyfriend. "That's not the issue here."

"Well, I for one am on your side," Amy assured Jessica. "But I have to admit I can't see the relationship lasting long. There are just too many obstacles. Society isn't ready for Cheryl and Steven—Sweet Valley isn't ready."

"It would be if you all took a more positive attitude," Jessica countered. "If you had as much guts as Cheryl and Steven!"

Shoving back her chair, she rose to her feet with dramatic dignity. It was time to show everyone just what she thought of her brother's risky romance with Cheryl Thomas!

Tossing back her hair, Jessica flounced over to the table where Cheryl was sitting with Elizabeth, Todd, Enid Rollins, Rosa Jameson, Annie, and Tony. She sensed that all eyes were on her; she was playing her new role to the hilt.

There was an empty chair next to Cheryl. Jessica dropped into it, then slipped an arm around Cheryl's shoulders and gave her a squeeze. Cheryl blinked at her in surprise. "I'm so happy for you and Steven," Jessica said loudly, so that the kids at neighboring tables could hear her. "We're going to have such a blast, now that you're officially a couple! I want to go on *lots* of double dates. And you have to come over to the house more often—you're practically a member of the family now."

Jessica's enthusiastic outburst left Cheryl speechless. "Uh, well . . ."

From across the table, Elizabeth caught Jessica's eye. Jessica knew what that look meant: *Don't be so pushy.* Jessica gave her twin another look in response: *Mind your own business!*

"Love is really in the air," she chattered on. "With your father and Mrs. Whitman's wedding coming up. . . . How romantic that you two will be together on that day!"

"Yeah," Cheryl agreed weakly.

47

"Don't you think it's romantic?" Jessica asked Annie and Tony.

Tony shrugged. Annie beamed. "It's very romantic. But I have to tell you, I get a headache when I think about the wedding. We still have so many details to take care of! Music for the ceremony, flowers, a cake . . . You can't have a wedding without a cake, can you?"

Jessica's eyes brightened with inspiration. "Liz and I would *love* to do something special for you and your parents," she blurted out. "We'll bake a wedding cake!"

Now Elizabeth was openly gaping at her twin. "A wedding cake?" she repeated. "Jessica, you can't even make a *pancake* without burning it!"

"That's absolutely not true," Jessica declared indignantly. "Don't listen to her, Annie and Cheryl."

"Listen to *me*," said Todd. "I've eaten Jessica's cooking and lived to tell the tale." He grinned. "Barely."

Elizabeth burst out laughing. Jessica scowled. "People always give me a hard time about being a crummy cook," she complained, "but it's a bum rap. I'm a perfectly good cook, and I just *know* I'll discover I have a flair for baking wedding cakes."

"You have a flair for culinary disaster," Todd mumbled.

"I'll buy a cookbook and follow the recipe. How hard can it be, especially if Liz helps me?" Jessica turned pleading eyes on Annie and Cheryl. "Please?"

Cheryl looked dubious, but Annie was clearly touched by the generous offer. "You made brownies once for a cheerleading-squad bake sale, and they were great," Annie remembered.

I used a mix, Jessica recalled, deciding now wasn't the time to reveal this.

"It *would* be special to have a cake baked by a friend," Annie went on, with a meaningful glance at Cheryl. "I mean, now that there's a *connection* between our two families. Thanks, Jessica!"

Jessica folded her arms across her chest, smiling smugly. Amy and the rest of the gang thought there were too many obstacles facing a couple like Steven and Cheryl. *Well, if that's the case, I'll just clear away a few of them,* Jessica thought with determination. *Anyone who makes trouble for Steven and Cheryl will have to answer to me!*

Five

Elizabeth bent over the desk, frowning at the typed sheet in front of her. *That first sentence still isn't right*, she fretted. She glanced over her shoulder in the hopes that Penny Ayala, *The Oracle*'s editor in chief, might still be around. But it was almost five o'clock, and the newspaper office had long since emptied out.

Just then, the door swung open. Jessica breezed in, dressed in the Lycra shorts and oversize T-shirt she had worn for cheerleading practice. "Ready to head home, Liz?"

With a frustrated sigh, Elizabeth shoved the unfinished article into a manila folder and stuck it in her shoulder bag. "As ready as I'll ever be," she replied.

She turned out the lights and made sure the office door was locked behind them. "So, what's the headline for the next issue of *The Oracle*?" Jessica asked as they strolled down the deserted hallway. " 'Cheryl Thomas Dates White Boy'? Or does the editorial staff think 'Steven Wakefield Falls for Black Girl' is catchier?"

"It seems to be the big story on campus," Elizabeth conceded with a grim smile.

They crossed the main lobby. Jessica pushed through the front door to the sidewalk. "I love to gossip, I'll admit it," she said. "But there's a line even I wouldn't cross. Some of the comments I overheard today really made me sick. I mean, people who are supposed to be Steven's and Cheryl's *friends*! Why is everybody so racist?"

Elizabeth brushed a strand of hair back from her face. She knew how Jessica felt; she had overheard some lousy things herself. "It can be discouraging," she agreed. "A lot of kids at school are pretty close-minded. But not *every*body."

"OK, not everybody," Jessica conceded grudgingly. "Too many, though. And I just don't get their attitude. Why can't they accept true love?"

"Whoa, slow down," Elizabeth advised. "True love? Cheryl and Steven have only known each other for about a month! I don't think we should assume something about them that might not be true."

"But Steven told us himself," Jessica reminded her twin. "They're romantically involved—they had their first kiss."

"Yeah, two whole days ago," Elizabeth pointed out. "All I'm saying is that relationships are fragile in the beginning, and this one may be even more so than most. Steven and Cheryl deserve some privacy.

51

With everything else that's going on, the last thing they need from you and me is a lot of pressure."

"Pressure? What pressure? What are you *talking* about?"

"I'm talking about lunch today." Elizabeth unlocked the Jeep and climbed into the driver's seat. "It's great to be supportive, Jess, but don't you think you overdid it with that sisterhood stuff? Cheryl seemed a little embarrassed."

"I didn't overdo it at all," Jessica retorted as she belted herself into the passenger seat. "Steven's our big brother. We have a *responsibility*, to him and to the whole world. We have to show *lots* of support. Do you want people to think we don't approve of Steven dating a black girl?"

Elizabeth stared at Jessica. "It's about loyalty, Liz, that's all," Jessica concluded quietly. "It's about doing what's right."

When Jessica puts it that way, it sounds so simple, Elizabeth thought as she started the Jeep's engine. *So why do I still have the nagging feeling that it is going to turn out to be anything but?*

"I like this place," Cheryl shouted to Rosa as they biked along the path skirting Secca Lake.

"Well, it *is* Sweet Valley's answer to Central Park," Rosa shouted back with a grin.

Cheryl had ridden over to Rosa's after school on Thursday. The Secca Lake recreation area, with its beaches, sports facilities, and nature trails, was only a short distance from the Jamesons' house on Honeysuckle Court, and Cheryl had never been there, so Rosa had steered them in that direction.

Now Cheryl braked her bicycle. Hopping down, she leaned the bike against a tree. "Let's walk by the lake," she suggested.

Scrambling down a stony, vine-tangled path, the two girls reached the sandy lakeshore. Cheryl bent to unlace her sneakers. "It's quiet here," she observed.

"It's less of a teen scene than the Pacific beaches," Rosa agreed.

"I'm glad I didn't give in to Annie's pressure to pledge PBA," Cheryl said.

"It wasn't the right sorority for either of us," Rosa agreed.

Cheryl strolled to the lake's edge, testing the water with her toe. "Although it would have been fun to see how they dealt with their newest member's shocking romance."

Rosa laughed. She raised one arm, pressing the back of her hand to her forehead in a dramatic fashion. "It would've sent them all into a swoon."

"I feel like I'm in a fishbowl as it is. I've felt that way ever since I moved to Sweet Valley, and it's worse than ever now."

"It'll pass," Rosa promised her. "All new couples get totally scrutinized. Pretty soon you and Steven will be yesterday's news."

"I don't know about that. A lot of people don't approve, and not all of them are going to come around. Prejudice has deep roots." Cheryl looked out over the sun-dappled lake, narrowing her eyes. "You know, what almost bothers me most is someone like Jessica."

"Jessica?" Rosa repeated in surprise. "But she's

really happy that you and Steven are going out. She told me so."

"She's *acting* happy about it," said Cheryl. "She's bending over backward to be nice to me. But I don't think she's sincere. She can't *really* like the idea of me dating her brother."

"Why would she pretend, then?"

"To cover up her prejudice," Cheryl guessed. "From me, and probably from herself too."

Rosa shook her head. "I know what it's like to be discriminated against, Cheryl, to be made to feel like you don't belong. Believe me. But I don't think you're being fair to Jessica. You've got to give her the benefit of the doubt. It's the only way to move ahead."

"It's just so hard!" Cheryl burst out in frustration. "When people are saying nasty things, and you know they're *thinking* worse."

Rosa's forehead creased in a sympathetic frown. "It is hard. But you know your friends—your real friends like me—are behind you one hundred percent. Anyhow, when it comes right down to it, the only thing that really matters is that you and Steven care for each other."

Cheryl stared at Rosa. "Me and Steven?"

Rosa laughed. "Yeah, silly, you and Steven! Isn't that what this is all about? What's in *your* hearts. What you two feel for each other, not what other people think or feel—that's what will determine whether the relationship works or not."

Cheryl turned away from Rosa and bent to pick up a flat stone. She didn't want her friend to see her face and witness her confusion. *Steven . . . what he and I feel for each other . . . What is in my heart?* Cheryl wondered.

All of a sudden, she realized that she didn't know. How *did* she really feel about Steven, and about the change in their relationship? She hadn't had time to think about it! She'd been too busy all week worrying about the public reaction.

Flicking the stone, Cheryl watched it skip across the silver surface of the lake. Steven . . . She focused on him with an effort, conjuring up the image of his face, the memory of his touch. She waited for the appropriate response. *I should be thrilled about seeing him again tomorrow night,* she thought. *I should shiver, remembering that kiss. That's what happens when you're in love with someone, right?*

Instead, Cheryl felt curiously empty and unmoved. She closed her eyes, concentrating, listening to her heart. She felt the breeze in her hair and the warmth of the sun on her skin; she heard the lap of the waves on the sand and the chatter of birds . . . nothing else.

It doesn't matter, she told herself firmly as she strode down the shore to catch up with Rosa, who had gone ahead. *I know what I'm doing and why I'm doing it. I'll show everybody—this relationship is going to work.* Cheryl thought of her father and Mona, planning to marry, pledging their love, despite the weight of social disapproval. *It has to work,* Cheryl vowed. *For all of us.*

"Don't bother with the dishes," Mona Whitman told Cheryl and Annie after supper on Friday. "Come into the studio and help me decide which engagement photo to submit to *The Sweet Valley News.*"

"The society page? Mom, that's so old-fashioned!" Annie teased.

"It's traditional," Mrs. Whitman corrected. She smiled. "Walter and I don't necessarily want to break *all* the rules."

Cheryl and Annie followed her down to the basement, which Mr. Thomas had converted into a photography studio and darkroom. Clipped to a clothesline was a row of black and white pictures of the whole family. Cheryl remembered the photo session a few weeks earlier. Her father had set up the camera on a tripod and used the automatic timer so that all four of them could be in the picture.

"I can't make up my mind," Mrs. Whitman said. "I like this one, but I also like that one. And this is a great shot. Don't we all look cute here?"

"But Mona, these are pictures of all four of us," Cheryl pointed out, puzzled. "You and Dad don't want me and Annie in your engagement picture!"

"Oh, yes, we do." Mona slung one arm around Cheryl's shoulders and the other around Annie. "Walter and I are bringing our lives together not just to make a marriage, but to make a family. You two are very much a part of what's going to happen two weeks from tomorrow."

A family . . . Tears of emotion stung Cheryl's eyes. For the first time, it really hit her; Mona was going to be her new mother. Cheryl was touched, but she was also unspeakably sad. Suddenly, her memories of her own mother seemed to fade, to recede into the distant past.

Cheryl stepped away, glad that Mrs. Whitman and Annie were hugging and couldn't see her face.

When they turned back to her, Cheryl had composed herself. "Sorry to be so mushy," Mona apologized. She wiped away a tear, laughing. "I guess I just wanted to make sure you girls knew how much it means to me and Walter that you'll be with us during the ceremony."

"I wanted to give away the bride, but I can settle for being a bridesmaid," Annie joked.

"Actually, there's another way you can participate," Mona told her. "It's traditional to give toasts at the wedding reception. Would you two each prepare a little speech?"

"I'd love to!" Annie hugged her mother again.

Cheryl smiled. "That sounds like fun."

"Great." Mona beamed. "So, back to the photos. What do you think?"

Cheryl tapped her pencil on the desk in her bedroom. The cool evening breeze ruffled the curtains at the open window; her eyes strayed from the blank sheet of paper in front of her. *A toast*, she mused. *What on earth am I going to say?*

Five minutes earlier, Annie had burst into Cheryl's bedroom to proclaim that she had already composed her toast. She was inspired—she sat right down and just wrote. She had read the toast to Cheryl, who had to agree that it was perfect.

Perfect for Annie, that is. With a sigh, Cheryl dropped the pencil and rested her chin in her hands, gazing out the window at the shadowy yard. Annie's toast was about love and family and living happily ever after. It was simple, sweet, and sincere. *This mixed-marriage, instant-family stuff seems easy for her at this point,* Cheryl thought. *But it's still not easy for me. How come?*

She didn't get a chance to reflect on the matter. There was a knock on her door. "Come on in," she called, assuming it was Annie again.

She turned in her chair. The door opened. "Steven!" Cheryl cried in surprise.

Steven smiled somewhat shyly. "Hope it's OK, barging in on you like this. Annie swore you were decent."

Cheryl laughed. "I'm dressed, anyway."

She got to her feet. Steven crossed the room. It was the first time they had seen each other since Sunday night, when they had stepped over the line separating platonic friendship from romance. *What should I do?* Cheryl wondered, suddenly feeling awkward and tongue-tied. *Kiss him? Shake his hand?*

Steven hesitated too. Reaching Cheryl's side, he put a hand on her shoulder. Then he bent to kiss her forehead just as she aimed for his cheek. They bumped heads.

As they both cracked up, Cheryl felt the tension between them dissipate. "Things are . . . different, huh?"

Steven pulled her to his side, giving her a friendly squeeze. "We'll get the hang of it."

Cheryl sat back down at her desk. Steven sat on the edge of the bed. "I bet you're glad it's the weekend," he remarked. "Last time we talked on the phone I got the impression that things had been kind of . . . stressful in school the last couple of days."

"I'm not letting it get to me. But, yeah," she had to admit. "I'm glad it's the weekend."

"What are you up to tonight? Am I interrupting anything?"

Cheryl shook her head. "I'm just trying to write a toast for Dad and Mona's wedding. Actually, maybe you could help me. I'm stuck."

"What have you got so far?"

Cheryl held up the blank sheet, smiling ruefully. "I really don't know where to begin. I guess my feelings are pretty complicated."

"Let's see . . ." Steven stroked his chin thoughtfully. "Well, how about starting with your first impression of all this? What did you think when they told you they were getting married?"

"I thought they were crazy." Cheryl grinned. "I thought they were nuts! But now—now I'm proud of them. It takes a lot of guts to swim against the tide."

"So, why don't you say something about that," Steven suggested.

"OK." Cheryl put the pencil to the page. She thought for a moment, then scribbled a sentence. "How does this sound? 'On this day, I'm very happy for my father and Mona Whitman. I'm also very proud of them for making a lifelong commitment to each other, despite the social forces arrayed against them.'" She wrinkled her nose. "That sounds kind of . . . dry."

"It's the right idea, though," Steven said.

"I can always reword it later," Cheryl agreed. "So now what?"

"Elaborate a little on that basic point. Talk about what it is that brought them together, what's going to *keep* them together."

What brought them together, what's going to keep them together . . . Cheryl tried to remember what had gone on between her father and Mrs. Whitman when they first met in New York City. Then she searched for words to describe their current contentment, their attitude toward the future. Instead, unrelated images flashed through Cheryl's brain. She saw herself with Steven at the Crooked Canyon Café, and then at the beach. . . .

Cheryl wrote quickly. Then she read her words aloud to Steven. " 'Many people stand ready to automatically condemn a relationship between two people of different races. A weak love can't survive the forces that seek to destroy it. Only a strong love that's bigger than social prejudice can endure. This is the kind of devotion my father and my new mother possess.' "

Steven nodded. "That's powerful."

"Hmm." Cheryl scanned the text. She frowned, dissatisfied. "Something's missing, though. There's still something I need to express. It's not complete."

"Why don't you end it by talking about the lesson we can all learn from Walter and Mona's example?" Steven suggested.

Cheryl jotted two more lines, finishing with a flourish. "There. All done!"

Pushing back her chair, she moved over to join Steven. Sitting side by side, they read the toast together in silence.

Cheryl waited for Steven's reaction. "I like it," he said at last.

"You don't sound totally thrilled," she commented.

"Well, now that I look at it . . ." Steven shrugged. "It's a minor thing. Just the tone, really."

"It's a little off. Like it's not quite right for a wedding, maybe?"

"Maybe," Steven said vaguely.

Cheryl stared at the paper, waiting for illumination. It didn't come. She shook her head, impatient. "It's fine for a first draft," she declared.

"It's a good start," Steven agreed heartily.

Cheryl folded the sheet crisply in two. "So," she said.

"So," Steven echoed.

They sat motionless for a moment. Then Steven wrapped his arms around her. For an instant, Cheryl stiffened. Then she hugged Steven back, tightly, to cover up her initial recoil.

When Steven bent his head to kiss her, Cheryl raised her mouth dutifully. His lips were warm; the kiss was tender and reassuring. Exactly as it should be. *So why do I feel distracted and weird?* Her own words repeated in her brain, forcing an unsettling reply. *Not quite right . . . not quite right . . . not quite right . . .*

Six

Steven raised himself on one elbow in bed, groping for the window. As he tugged own the shade, the cord slipped through his fingers and the shade shot all the way up with a snap. Steven squeezed his eyes shut against the bright morning sun. "So much for sleeping in," he grunted. He sat up and swung his legs over the side of the bed, glancing at the clock-radio on his nightstand. Eleven o'clock —well, maybe that was late enough to be lazing in bed on a gorgeous Saturday.

He pulled on a pair of sweatpants and then shuffled downstairs. Jessica was sitting at the kitchen table in her bathrobe, her hair tousled and her eyes still squinty with sleep. "I'm glad to see I'm not the only lazy bum in this house," Steven greeted her.

Jessica yawned. "Ditto. The rest of the gang's been up for *hours*. It's sickening."

Steven looked out into the backyard. His parents were working in the garden; Elizabeth had camped out at the picnic table with a stack of books. "What a guilt trip," he agreed.

"Well, I don't let it get to me." Jessica spooned into a slice of cantaloupe. "I think it should be against the law to be productive on Saturday."

Steven poured himself a cup of coffee. "I hear you, Jess."

"Still." She gave him the eye. "I'm surprised *you* wasted so much time sleeping. Aren't you doing stuff with Cheryl today?"

"Uh, yeah, I suppose so."

"I mean, all you two *have* is the weekends. You've got to make the most of it! Spend every minute together!"

Steven winced. "You sound like you're about to break into a cheer," he said dryly. "Go, team, go."

"I'm just happy." Jessica dimpled. "It's a blast being part of a couple, isn't it?"

A couple. That's right. Steven sipped his coffee, contemplating the idea. He and Cheryl were now a couple. So it was a given fact that they would do everything together, go out every Saturday night. *A couple* ... For some inexplicable reason, Steven suddenly found himself wishing he had an excuse to head back to campus early.

"I mean, before I started seeing Sam, I thought it was better to be single," Jessica chattered. "To go out with one guy on Friday and someone else on Saturday. I didn't want to be tied down. But once I met Sam ... Well, *you* know."

Steven wasn't sure he did, but he nodded anyway.

"This is going to be a big night for you and Cheryl," Jessica remarked as she spread apricot jam on a piece of toast.

Steven lifted his eyebrows. "How so?"

"It's your first public appearance as a couple!" His sister seemed astonished that he could be unaware of the magnitude of this occasion. "So, what are you going to do?' she prodded. "Dinner? Dancing?"

Our first public appearance, dinner, dancing . . . The memory of his and Cheryl's impromptu dinner date at the Crooked Canyon Café the previous weekend flared painfully in Steven's consciousness. The desire to skip town grew even stronger.

Just then, Elizabeth pushed open the screen door. "Morning, guys."

"Hi, Liz. Hey, by the way, what are you and Todd doing tonight?" Steven asked on a sudden impulse. "Want to double with Cheryl and me?"

"We're going to a party in Big Mesa with Enid and Hugh," Elizabeth answered regretfully as she took a pitcher of orange juice from the fridge. "Some other time, OK?"

Steven turned to Jessica. "How about you and Sam?"

"We'd love to, but we already made dinner plans with Amy and Barry," Jessica told Steven. "Maybe next weekend."

"Sure. Next weekend."

Elizabeth headed back outside with a glass of juice; still yawning, Jessica drifted upstairs to change into her bathing suit. Steven remained at the table, drumming his fingers. Then he picked up the telephone and punched in some numbers.

"Hello," a groggy male voice said.

"Hey, Bob. Did I wake you up?"

"As a matter of fact, you did," Steven's college roommate replied. "Lucky for you, I was about to get up anyway—there's an intramural softball game in half an hour. What's happening?"

"I'm checking to see if you feel like road tripping to Sweet Valley tonight. I thought maybe we could get a bunch of people together, go dancing or something. You can meet Cheryl."

"Cheryl. The girl from New York, right?"

"Right. So what do you say?"

Bob contemplated the proposal. "Sure," he said at last. "I'm up for it."

"Great. Round up Eve and Beth, too, OK? And I'll call Frazer and Hillary. We'll look for you at the Beach Disco at nine."

Hanging up with Bob, Steven dialed Frazer McConnell's number. No one was home, but Frazer's answering machine picked up. Steven left a message. He was about to replace the receiver when he thought of someone else. He dialed one more number.

"Hey, Martin," he said when Martin Bell answered the phone. "It's Steve."

"Steve, what's up?" Martin replied. "Are you on campus? I thought Bob said you went home for the weekend."

"I am home," Steven told him. "I'm just trying to drum up some action for tonight. Bob, Beth, and

65

Eve are driving down, and hopefully Frazer and Hillary too. How about you? Will you be in the mood for some good food and great music?"

"That's my favorite combo," Martin said with a chuckle. "I'll hitch a ride with Frazer and Hillary."

Steven hung up the telephone. His coffee had cooled in the cup, so he dumped it out and poured a fresh, hot refill. He felt absurdly glad, relieved even, that his friends would be joining him and Cheryl that evening. How come?

Narrowing his eyes against the sunlight, Steven gazed pensively out at the swimming pool. Now that he thought about it, what he had just done was pretty weird. He'd just entered into a new romance—he should be dying for time alone with Cheryl. Instead, he had gone out of his way to organize a group outing.

One possible explanation flickered in his brain. *I'm not afraid to be alone with her*, he told himself firmly. But he couldn't forget the hostility of the skinheads at the Crooked Canyon Café. No two ways about it, he did *not* want to get himself or Cheryl into a situation like that again.

An even more unsettling thought struck him. *Is that why I called Martin?* Steven wondered. So there would be another black person in the group, so Cheryl wouldn't stand out so much? *Naw*, he decided. He really didn't think of Martin as black; they were pals, on the same I.M. basketball and soccer teams, and both prelaw.

Finally, one last explanation presented itself to Steven, and he felt more comfortable with this one. It wasn't that he was avoiding intimacy with Cheryl—

he just wanted to show her off to his friends. Nothing strange about that. *That's it*, Steven concluded, gulping a mouthful of coffee and shoving the other, more disturbing speculations from his mind.

Jessica stuck her head out past Elizabeth's bedroom door. "Have a great time," she shouted down the hall after her brother. "Don't do anything I wouldn't do!"

"Thanks for leaving me so much slack," Steven yelled back.

Elizabeth ran a brush through her glossy blond hair. "I thought he'd never leave," she commented.

"He fussed about what shirt to wear for hours," Jessica agreed. She mimicked Steven's deep voice. " 'Did I overdo it with the aftershave? How's my hair? Do these socks match?' "

Elizabeth laughed. "He was a nervous wreck."

"You'd think he'd never gone on a date before," Jessica added, disappearing into the bathroom that connected the twins' bedrooms.

Elizabeth slipped her feet into a pair of black sandals and tightened the belt around her slim waist. Then she crossed the bedroom to check her reflection in the full-length mirror on the back of her door. The short, turquoise-blue dress had a gently scooped neckline; the gold lavaliere she always wore sparkled against her bare throat. *Todd likes this dress*, Elizabeth reflected, her cheeks turning pink as she anticipated the admiring look—and the kiss—with which he was sure to greet her. *It's always a good choice!*

Elizabeth cut through the bathroom to Jessica's room. Her sister was standing in front of her closet in her underwear. "I have nothing to wear!" Jessica moaned.

"Nothing to *wear*?" Elizabeth pointed to the avalanche of clothing spilling from the closet. "What do you call that?"

Jessica kicked morosely at the pile of clothing at her feet. "Laundry."

Elizabeth laughed. "Jessica, you have more clothes than most department stores. You must have *something* that's clean."

Jessica pulled a red knit minidress from the rack. She wrinkled her nose at it. "I'm pretty sure I wore this two weekends ago when Sam and I drove up to Marpa Heights for dinner."

"How about that?" Elizabeth pointed to a white twill miniskirt.

"I'm positive I wore that last weekend." Jessica heaved a defeated sigh. Then her eyes brightened. "But maybe if I borrowed something of *yours* to wear on top . . ."

"Jess!"

"Pretty please?"

Jessica batted her eyelashes. Elizabeth couldn't help smiling. "Oh, all right."

The twins trooped back to Elizabeth's room. While Jessica riffled through her dresser drawers, Elizabeth sat on the bed, her expression suddenly thoughtful. "Jess," she said after a moment, "do you think it's weird that Steven was so nervous about going out with Cheryl tonight?"

Jessica faced the mirror, holding a cropped orange T-shirt against herself. "Weird? Not at all. It just proves how much he likes her."

"So you don't think it was kind of strange that he asked you and me if we wanted to double-date with them tonight."

Jessica shook her head. "Of course not." Tossing the T-shirt aside, she reached for a pink cotton sweater. "That was just his way of letting us know that he's serious about Cheryl; that he wants us to accept the two of them as a couple—which I'm taking every opportunity to assure him we do." Discarding the sweater, Jessica grabbed a brightly striped tank top. She waved the shirt at Elizabeth. "Thanks for the loan. Have fun at the party!"

Alone again, Elizabeth continued to think about Steven . . . and Cheryl. Something about her brother's new romance troubled her. Elizabeth frowned. *Am I less tolerant than I think I am?* she challenged herself. *Is it because Cheryl's black?*

Elizabeth stared the question in the face. Then she sighed. That wasn't it. She had absolutely nothing against Cheryl—she would approve of any girl who made Steven happy. *But is he happy?* Elizabeth wondered. And this time, she didn't know the answer.

"I hope it's OK with you that I invited some other people along tonight," Steven said to Cheryl as he parked at the Beach Disco.

Walking around the car, he held the door open for Cheryl. She stepped out of the VW. "Of course it's OK," she assured him.

Immediately, she worried that she had sounded

too glad. She didn't want Steven to guess how relieved she was that some of his buddies would be showing up, that they wouldn't be alone. "I'm looking forward to meeting your college friends," she added casually.

"Good. Because there they are."

Steven took Cheryl's hand and led her toward a small cluster of people standing near the entrance of the oceanside restaurant and dance club, one of the most popular weekend night spots for young people in Sweet Valley.

Is he nervous introducing his new black girlfriend to his white college pals? Cheryl wondered. He must have warned them—no one blinked at the sight of her. It was Cheryl who blinked. To her surprise, she saw that Steven's friends *weren't* all white.

"Cheryl, I'd like you to meet my wild and crazy roommate, Bob Rose," Steven said. "And Eve Young and Beth Greenberg—they're roommates in the next dorm. This is Martin Bell—he's in my pre-law study group. And last but not least, Hillary and Frazer. Everybody, this is Cheryl Thomas."

Cheryl shook hands all around, smiling. "Nice to see you all."

"I hope you like to dance, Cheryl," Frazer said to her as they headed inside. "Because the music here is hot."

"I love to dance," she replied.

Frazer turned to Steven. "You're going to have to share her, you know."

Hillary took hold of Steven's arm, winking at Cheryl. "And *she's* going to have to share *him*."

Cheryl smiled. "I think we can deal with that."

They found an empty table at the edge of the outdoor dance floor and ordered some appetizers. As the conversation among the university students turned to the results of that day's intramural games, Cheryl felt herself relaxing. All afternoon she had been tense, dreading this first official date with Steven and the public scrutiny it was bound to entail. Now she tapped her foot to the music, her eyes scanning the crowd for familiar Sweet Valley High faces. *Maybe this isn't going to be so bad after all.*

"Ready to put some mileage on those dancing shoes?" someone asked.

Cheryl looked up. Martin stood by her chair, smiling down at her.

Cheryl put down her glass of punch and returned his smile. "Sure."

Martin guided her onto the dance floor, his hand cupped lightly against the small of her back. An unexpected shiver chased up Cheryl's spine.

It's a cool night, she thought, darting a glance at Martin. But she felt another electric tingle when they faced each other and she got her first long look at him. His baggy black cotton trousers and T-shirt accentuated his lean, broad-shouldered build; he had the kind of casual but elegant style that Cheryl always fell for. And he was *tall*. She had to look up to meet his intense dark eyes, and for some reason as she did so she felt a little dizzy.

The song had a moderate beat—neither fast nor slow. Martin clasped one of Cheryl's hands and curved his other arm lightly around her waist. He didn't pull her close, but he didn't hold her at a distance, either.

71

They began swaying to the music. "I like this song," Cheryl said, surprised to find herself somewhat breathless.

"Eddie's R & B Express," Martin told her. "My favorite band. I once took a saxophone lesson from Eddie himself."

Cheryl was impressed. "Really?"

Martin grinned wryly. "Well, in a matter of speaking. The Express was playing at a club near school, and I caught Eddie in between sets. In the men's room," he added. Cheryl laughed. "He gave me a couple tips."

"So, you play the saxophone."

Martin swung Cheryl around, then dipped her. She laughed again. "Yep. I play with a little jazz combo at school—frat parties and the like. We earn pizza money, that's about it, but it's fun."

"I'd love to hear you play," Cheryl said impulsively.

"I'll make sure you get a chance," Martin vowed. "One of these days when you come up to campus to visit Steven."

Steven. Cheryl's cheeks burned with sudden chagrin. She hoped Martin couldn't read her expression. *Steven. I almost forgot about him!*

Martin didn't seem to notice her discomfort. "Steven tells me you're a musician too," he remarked.

Cheryl nodded. "Piano. Classical, mostly, but some jazz."

"We'll have to try a duet sometime," Martin suggested.

Cheryl felt herself blush again. "Sure," she said weakly.

The song faded out. Cheryl and Martin stepped apart, but for a moment their fingers remained entwined. Then Martin dropped her hand. With reluctance? Cheryl wondered. Or was it just her imagination, wishful thinking?

"Thanks for the dance," Martin said. "That was fun."

Too much fun! Cheryl thought with a pang of guilt as she looked around for Steven.

"Look at them," Jessica urged Sam as her boyfriend swung her around the dance floor at the Beach Disco. "Are they madly in love or what?"

Sam nuzzled Jessica's neck. "How about paying some attention to me for a change?" he suggested. "I'm madly in love too, you know."

Jessica gave Sam a perfunctory peck on the cheek, then turned her attention back to Steven and Cheryl. "I mean, they've both danced a couple of songs with other people, but it's totally obvious they can't wait to get back to each other," she observed. "It's like there's some irresistible magnetic force between them."

Sam squeezed Jessica. "I know *that* feeling."

Jessica twisted just as he zeroed in for a kiss. Sam's lips landed on the back of her hair. "Hey, Amy," Jessica called over her shoulder.

Amy steered Barry around so she could better talk to Jessica. "You caught me staring," she confessed. "Your brother and Cheryl make a gorgeous couple."

"I know," said Jessica. "I can't believe Steven was actually nervous about this date!"

"They're taking Sweet Valley by storm. Well, *most* of Sweet Valley," Amy added with a glance at a nearby table.

Still bobbing to the music, Jessica propelled Sam over to the table where Lila was sitting. "Hasn't anybody asked you to dance, Miss Wallflower?"

Lila scowled. "No one I'd touch with a ten-foot pole."

"Too bad," Jessica replied. "Because love is really in the air tonight."

"Love." Lila snorted disdainfully, her eyes on Steven and Cheryl. "Is that what you call it?"

"Watch it, Li," Jessica warned.

"Well, I guess there's no law against two people dancing together," Lila drawled. "Maybe to some people, Steven and Cheryl represent the newest fad. But take my word for it, Jessica. Lots of people won't go for it."

"*Snobs* won't go for it," Jessica retorted. "It's not a question of fashion, anyway. Take *my* word for it. You're going to end up all by yourself on this one, Li."

Lila raised her eyebrows. "Do you really think so? Then maybe we attended different Sweet Valley Highs last week. I didn't get the impression that everyone feels the way you do about this—far from it."

"People can change their minds," Jessica insisted, surprising herself by the depth of her own conviction. "People can grow."

Lila smiled cynically. "We'll see."

"*You'll* see," Jessica predicted.

* * *

"You have more energy than me," Cheryl said to Steven later that evening. "I think I'm about danced out."

"Just one more song," Steven urged. He pulled her body close to his. "This one's slow. It shouldn't take too much out of you."

Biting her lip, Cheryl rested her head gingerly against Steven's chest. *One more dance*, she told herself. *Just try to relax.*

But she couldn't. As she and Steven began to dance, Cheryl's eyes wandered around the dance floor. She glimpsed a bunch of people she knew from school: Jessica and Sam, Amy and Barry, DeeDee Gordon and Bill Chase, Ken Matthews and Terri Adams, and Bruce Patman and his latest fling, a curvy blond sophomore named Chelsea. It was her and Steven's first night out since word got around that they were an item, and all night, people had been looking curiously their way. Strangers were gawking too. *Reason enough to feel awkward*, Cheryl concluded. But was that *really* the explanation?

Her eyes drifted to another couple dancing nearby. Martin and Eve had their arms wrapped around each other in a friendly manner and they were talking up a storm. Martin's face was so animated, so handsome. . . .

Cheryl fought back the traitorous rush of feeling. But it was there—she couldn't deny it. Practically from the moment she met him, she had felt a strong attraction to Martin Bell. She had danced with him twice, and she had enjoyed it far more than her dances with Frazer and Bob . . . more even than her dances with Steven.

Cheryl looked anxiously up at Steven, as if hoping to find the answer to this puzzle in his face. He caught her eye and smiled. She smiled back, then turned her face away again so they wouldn't have to talk.

I'm not attracted to Steven, Cheryl realized with a shock. *I don't have that kind of feeling for him.* Suddenly, she understood why she had felt uncomfortable being near him the previous evening when he stopped by her house. Talking was one thing, but she didn't enjoy it when he put his arms around her; she didn't *really* want him to kiss her. Something romantic had passed between them on the beach under the stars. But now, a week later, Steven's touch simply left her cold.

But I'm in love with Steven, Cheryl thought, her emotions in a state of complete confusion. *What's going on here?*

Moving mechanically to the music, Cheryl struggled to analyze her feelings. She felt a physical attraction to Martin, but not to Steven. Why? There was one obvious explanation—she had to face it head-on. *Am I attracted to Martin because he's black, and not attracted to Steven because he's white?*

Cheryl tightened her arms around Steven, remembering how he had stood by her at the Crooked Canyon Café, how he had been her good, true friend from the very beginning. *No,* she thought as Steven brushed the top of her head with his lips. *It can't be that.*

"Hey, you two," Frazer called when the song ended. "It's getting late. I think we're going to hit the road."

Cheryl drew away from Steven. "Ready to take off?" he asked her. She nodded. "Then let's walk those guys out to the parking lot."

All six of Steven's friends had ridden down in Frazer's secondhand Volvo. Before they squeezed back into the car, Bob slapped Steven on the back. "See you back at the dorm tomorrow night, right?"

"Right," Steven confirmed.

"It was nice meeting you, Cheryl," Hillary said with a warm smile.

Cheryl waved good-bye to the girls as they piled into the car. Then, irresistibly, her eyes moved to Martin, who stood just a few feet away, his hands in his trouser pockets.

Martin met her gaze and held it. "Congratulations, folks," he said. "Steve, you're a lucky guy."

Steven wrapped an arm firmly around Cheryl's shoulders. "I know it."

Cheryl couldn't speak. She dropped her eyes to the pavement, positive she had never felt quite so awkward . . . or quite so guilty.

Seven

"This is your last chance, kiddo," Mr. Thomas called to Cheryl from the front hallway. "Sure you don't want a ride to the beach? We could grab Steven on our way out."

Cheryl rested her hands lightly on the keys of the piano in the living room. "Thanks anyway, Dad," she yelled back. "I have a history test tomorrow. I need to study."

She heard the door slam.

With her right hand, Cheryl picked out a tune on the piano. Her dark eyes grew dreamy. The song had a seductive, danceable rhythm. . . .

Cheryl frowned, wondering. *How do I know this melody?* The answer registered in her brain with a click: it was the bluesy song she had danced to with Martin Bell at the Beach Disco the night before.

Slamming the piano lid shut, Cheryl jumped to her feet. She grabbed her history textbook and sunglasses from the coffee table and rushed out to the deck.

The late morning sun was intense. Cheryl hoisted one of the lounge chairs and dragged it off the deck into the shade of an orange tree. Settling into the chair, she adjusted her sunglasses and opened the book to the chapter on the Civil War.

It was a period in American history that Cheryl found fascinating, but today she couldn't seem to keep any of the dates, events, or people straight. *Dred Scott . . . the Compromise of 1850 . . . the Missouri Compromise . . . I can't think.* Cheryl closed her eyes, letting her head drop back. *I can't think about history, anyway. I need to think about me right now. I need to think about my life. It's a mess!*

With a sigh, Cheryl opened her eyes—just in time to see Steven striding toward her across the lawn. *So much for privacy,* Cheryl thought with a sharp twinge of irritation. *So much for time to myself.* Why couldn't Steven live on the other side of town instead of right next door?

Steven smiled broadly at her. Cheryl bit her lip, swamped by a wave of guilt. Steven was such a sweet, wonderful guy. How could she have had such a nasty thought about him?

"You look so cool and comfortable." Steven dropped down onto the grass next to her chair. "I had to come over and bug you."

"I needed a distraction—you're just in time," Cheryl fibbed. "I'm having a hard time getting into the mood for American history."

Steven leaned back on his hands. "I had a good time last night," he said, his eyes on her face.

Cheryl forced a smile, glad that she had sunglasses on so Steven couldn't see the expression in her eyes. "Yeah. Me too."

"I'll miss you this week, when I'm back at school," Steven went on. He stretched out his arm, idly brushing the back of his hand along the side of Cheryl's calf.

Cheryl's back stiffened. She shifted in her chair, moving out of range of Steven's touch. *This is wrong*, she thought. *All wrong*.

"Steven," Cheryl said out loud. "There's something I need to talk to you about."

"What is it?"

Cheryl hesitated. What should she say? Should she tell him that she was all mixed up, that she had feelings for another guy, one of his own friends? Cheryl contemplated Steven's expectant face. He was such a good person. All at once, she wished vehemently that they could go back in time, to when they were just friends. She was so much more comfortable with him then! She wasn't sure why that was the case—not that it mattered. They couldn't go back. She had to deal with the situation they were currently in.

"You see, it's about . . ." Cheryl searched for the right words. Why was it so hard to find them? "I wonder if—"

"Hey, Cheryl!" somebody shouted.

Cheryl turned to see Annie sticking her head out past the sliding glass door. "What is it?" Cheryl asked, half annoyed and half relieved by the interruption.

"Mom and I are going shopping," Annie replied.

"To look for wedding and bridesmaid dresses. Wanna come?"

"Be right there," Cheryl called. She turned back to Steven. "I really can't skip this trip. If I leave it up to Annie, we'll end up wearing pink."

Steven laughed. "A fate worse than death."

Cheryl rose to her feet, dropping the history textbook onto the lounge chair. "So . . . I guess I'll see you later."

"We can squeeze in one more driving lesson before I head back to campus," Steven agreed. "But what did you want to talk about?"

"Oh . . ." They didn't have time to get into a heavy-duty conversation now, and maybe that was just as well. Maybe she didn't want to break up with Steven, after all. She would hate to jeopardize their friendship. And what would everyone think? Cheryl imagined the school gossips like Lila Fowler and Caroline Pearce gloating over her failure. People would say the breakup was inevitable. The whole town would take it as a sign that interracial romance couldn't work.

And it can work. Cheryl's heart flooded with hope and determination. *Steven and I will prove it.*

She smothered her doubts about Steven; she simply wouldn't give into them. Rising on tiptoe, she kissed Steven's cheek lightly. "It was nothing much. I just wanted to ask for your help with my wedding toast again. I'm thinking about revising it."

"We'll work on it tonight," Steven promised.

Jessica held up a huge stainless-steel cake pan and grimaced. "I'd rather be looking at wedding

81

dresses with Annie and Cheryl and Mrs. Whitman," she complained.

Elizabeth put her hands on her hips. "Look, it was your idea to bake this cake. Do you want to go over to the Designer Shop and tell Mrs. Whitman you don't want to do it after all? They're still there."

Jessica glanced over her shoulder. The Designer Shop was located right across the mall from the Creative Cook where she and Elizabeth were shopping; she could see Annie and Cheryl oohing and aahing as Mrs. Whitman modeled a floaty white dress for them. Jessica sighed. "No, a promise is a promise. It's just that these pans are so *big*. You could swim laps in this thing!"

Elizabeth grinned. "How did you *think* you made a three-tiered wedding cake, by piling three cupcakes on top of each other?"

"No," Jessica said haughtily. She wasn't about to admit that she had been hoping to come across a wedding-cake mix, maybe something you could whip up in the microwave. "OK, if you're so smart, which recipe should we go with?"

She knew she had stumped her twin with that one. Elizabeth picked up the stack of cookbooks they had located and weighed them in her hands, as if to come up with an answer that way. "I really have no idea," she confessed.

"Well, I guess we'll just have to buy them all," Jessica declared impatiently. Usually she loved shopping, but this was more like working toward a Girl Scout badge. "Come on, let's get this over with!"

A few minutes later they emerged from the Creative Cook, each lugging a shopping bag, and nearly collided with Bruce Patman. Jessica made a sour face, as if she smelled something rotten. Of all people to run into, her least favorite classmate, Bruce, the arrogant, aristocratic idiot.

"Why, hello, ladies," Bruce said in his most patronizing tone. "Stocking up on pots and pans, eh? I'm truly delighted to discover this domestic tendency, especially in *you*, Jessica."

"We'd rather be domestic than qualify as a zoo animal like you, Bruce," Jessica retorted.

Elizabeth nodded at the three tennis rackets Bruce was carrying. "Taking those to be restrung?"

"Actually, these are new." Bruce swung one of the rackets, striking an athletic pose. "I don't have time to sit around waiting for my rackets to be restrung. My game is too important and my time is too valuable."

Jessica yawned. Bruce never missed a chance to remind people that in addition to being a star of the Sweet Valley High tennis team, he also happened to be the wealthiest boy in town. Obnoxious, unsubtle boasting came as naturally to him as breathing did. "Well, I sure wish I could watch you play," she said sarcastically. "You hold a racket in each hand and the third one between your teeth, right?"

Elizabeth giggled. "Now, that would be something to see."

Bruce lifted one dark eyebrow, his expression the epitome of disdain. "You'd better get on home to your stove," he rejoined.

Jessica prepared to stomp off, but her foot came

out of her sandal and she tripped. The shopping bag flew from her arms, its contents spilling all over the floor.

"Here, let me help you," Bruce said with mock gallantry. He picked up one of the cookbooks, reading the title out loud. "*Wonderful Wedding Cakes.* What's this for?"

Jessica snatched the book from him. "For your information," she answered haughtily, "Liz and I, who have a reputation around town as excellent cooks, have been asked by Annie's mother and Cheryl's father to bake their wedding cake."

"What a privilege," said Bruce, his tone snide and insinuating. "These black-white liaisons certainly seem to be the latest thing."

Jessica put her hands on her hips. "Are you trying to make a point, Bruce?"

"Not really," he drawled. "But I saw your brother out with Cheryl last night. You must be *very* proud of the spectacle he's making of himself."

"As a matter of fact, we are proud of him," Elizabeth declared.

"You're just jealous," Jessica accused, "because you know Cheryl Thomas wouldn't go out with *you* if you were the last man on earth."

Bruce grinned, lifting a tennis racket in an ironic salute. "Have fun baking your cake. Don't forget, at least half of it should be *chocolate.*"

Bruce sauntered off. Elizabeth shook her head, utterly disgusted. "Is it my imagination, or is he more of a pig than ever?"

"It's not your imagination," Jessica assured her. "But we're doing the animal kingdom a disfavor by saying he belongs in a zoo or a barn. He's not an animal—he's pond scum."

"I almost feel sorry for that girl he's going out with," Elizabeth said as they headed for the Mall exit. "What's her name—Bettina."

"Bettina was last week," Jessica reported. "This week it's Chelsea. And next week it'll be some other poor unsuspecting bimbo. Good ol' Bruce— he goes through girls even faster than he goes through tennis rackets!"

The twins pulled into the driveway just as Sam was hopping off his dirt bike. Jessica sprang from the Jeep. Sprinting over to her boyfriend, she tackled him to the grass with a giant bear hug.

"Hey, I thought we were on the same team!" Sam protested.

Jessica pinned him on his back, then kissed him. "I'm calling a time-out."

Sam wrapped his arms around her, grinning. "OK, let's huddle."

Jessica held him close. "I'm just so glad you're *you* and not Bruce Patman," she explained.

"I have absolutely no idea where that comment came from, but I'm glad too," said Sam.

Elizabeth dropped the shopping bags on the lawn next to them. Jessica and Sam disentangled themselves. Sam reached into one of the bags and pulled out a strange-looking gadget. He aimed it at Elizabeth. "Choose your weapon, Liz. What *is* this thing, by the way?"

She laughed. "It's for making flowers with cake frosting."

Jessica dumped out the other shopping bag. Cookbooks tumbled onto the lawn. "It's really not a laughing matter," she chided her boyfriend. "With all these different methods, how are we supposed to know where to start?"

Sam flipped open a cookbook and examined a color photo of an elaborately decorated wedding cake. "Hey, I have an idea," he said, his eyes twinkling.

"What?" Jessica asked.

"The best way to make a perfect wedding cake for Mrs. Whitman and Mr. Thomas is to practice first. Experiment a little—bake a couple of sample cakes." Sam rubbed his hands together and licked his lips. "Todd and I would be more than happy to act as your official tasters and let you know when you have a winner."

Jessica tackled him again. "I *bet* you'd be happy! Sounds to *me* like a scheme for you to stuff your faces."

"Fine. If you don't want my help . . ." Sam dropped the cookbooks onto Jessica's lap. "Good luck."

"You know, Jess, maybe it's not such a bad idea." Elizabeth held out a hand and hauled her twin up. "Let's get to work. I have a feeling we're going to need all the practice we can get!"

"I did it!" Cheryl cried excitedly. "I parallel-parked! Did you see me? I backed right into that space like I've been doing it all my life. I didn't bump the other cars once."

"It's a small space too." Steven grinned. "And

look at that—we're right up against the curb. I don't have to jump!"

They got out of the car and walked down the sidewalk toward Guido's Pizza Palace—they had decided to grab some dinner before Steven headed back to school. "Pretty soon you're not going to need any more driving lessons," he remarked.

Cheryl looked over at Steven quickly. Her conscience stabbed her. *Did he notice something was wrong this morning? Did he guess what was on my mind?*

Steven held the restaurant door open for Cheryl. "You'll get your license," he continued, "and then you can come up to campus for a change."

"Right," Cheryl said, relieved.

The hostess picked up a couple of menus as they approached. "Table for two?" she inquired, looking from Steven to Cheryl.

The hostess's manner was perfectly friendly, but Cheryl bristled anyway. "Table for two," she affirmed, reaching out to clasp Steven's hand firmly in her own.

They received a few desultory glances on the way to their table, next to the artificial waterfall. They sat down across from each other and this time he took her hand, squeezing it warmly. "For you, *ma chérie*," Steven murmured, "I'll abstain from pepperoni. Should we try the vegetarian special with extra cheese?"

Cheryl smiled. *"Mais oui."*

They started out with an antipasto plate. As they dug in hungrily, Steven reminded Cheryl of something. "We were going to work on your toast for the wedding, remember?"

87

"That's right." Cheryl took a small notepad and a pen from her shoulder bag. "I tossed out what we wrote a couple nights ago," she confessed. "I just wasn't happy with it. You felt it too, remember? The tone—it was off somehow. So we have to start over. I want it to be *perfect*."

"I understand," said Steven. "So, let's have another go at it."

"OK." Cheryl looked at him, her pen poised. Out of the corner of her eye, she was aware that the elderly couple at the next table were watching them with undisguised interest. "It just shouldn't matter," Cheryl burst out suddenly, loud enough for the old people to hear. "It shouldn't matter that Dad's black and Mona's white. That's what this marriage is all about, if you ask me. It's about showing the world that it's OK for two people to love each other even though their skins are a different color. We should *all* love each other."

"We have a responsibility," Steven affirmed.

Cheryl bent her head, writing rapidly. Then she passed the notebook to Steven. "Tell me honestly what you think."

Steven read the toast. "I think it's good," he said after a moment. "Meaningful."

Silently, Cheryl reread her own words. *Strangers might look at my father and Mona Whitman and assume they don't belong together. An interracial couple, in some people's opinion, is a classic case of 'What's wrong with this picture?' But by exchanging wedding vows today, my father and my new stepmother demonstrate that there's nothing wrong with the picture. The problem, if there is one, is with the viewer.*

88

Meaningful, Cheryl mused. *Maybe. But does it mean what I want it to mean?*

"I don't know," she said doubtfully. "It still sounds kind of . . . *academic.*"

"In that case, I give it an *A*," Steven joked.

Cheryl slipped the notebook into her purse. *I give it an F*, she thought, stifling a discontented sigh.

Her feelings must have shown on her face. Steven took her hand again. "Cheryl, I know this is really important to you. Just remember, words aren't the only way we communicate with the world. It's not just what we say that matters, but what we do, how we live."

Cheryl nodded. Steven was right. She thought of the challenge facing her dad and Annie's mom; she thought of that fateful night with Steven just a week ago when they stopped at the Crooked Canyon Café. Then she thought about her response to Martin Bell at the Beach Disco the night before.

What really matters is what we do and how we live. . . . It was the truth, and Cheryl wasn't about to let herself forget it. She took Steven's hand, pushing Martin's image out of her mind. She wasn't going to take the easy way out.

Eight

"Hi, Cheryl," Jessica said as she and Lila stepped into the lunch line behind her on Monday.

Cheryl turned, a carton of strawberry yogurt in her hand. She smiled. "Hi, Jessica."

The smile didn't last long, Jessica noted. When Cheryl's eyes met Lila's, her expression cooled. "Hi, Lila," she said flatly.

Lila lifted her chin. "Why, hello, Cheryl," she responded in a tone that somehow managed to be too polite. "Did you have a good time at the Beach Disco on Saturday night? You were certainly dancing up a storm."

"You know what they say about my people," Cheryl replied dryly. "We've got rhythm."

She turned her back abruptly on Lila. Placing the yogurt on her tray, she considered a display of fresh fruit. "The apples look good today," Jessica commented helpfully, hoping Cheryl wouldn't associate her with Lila's rudeness.

"You're right." Cheryl chose a big, shiny red apple. "Well, see ya, Jessica."

Cheryl paid for her lunch and headed across the cafeteria to a table by the windows where Rosa was sitting. That left only one empty table, just two tables away; Lila made a beeline for it. Tray in hand, Jessica trailed after Lila.

Or should I sit with Cheryl? Jessica wondered. She wavered; it was a tough choice. Her best friend or her brother's new girlfriend? Finally, she set her tray down next to Lila's. *I'll talk some sense into her*, Jessica figured.

She stuck a straw in her bottle of apple juice. "You know, you should really make more of an effort to be civil to Cheryl, Li," Jessica remarked.

"Why?" Lila asked before biting into her tuna-in-pita-bread sandwich. "She wasn't so civil to the PBAs, turning us down the way she did. Beside, she's not *my* sister-in-law."

"You're just being stubborn," Jessica pursued. "You don't really care who my brother goes out with. You're just negative about *all* couples these days, and you feel like you have to stick to your original opinion about interracial ones."

Lila raised her slender eyebrows at Jessica. "You don't know the first thing about what I feel," she stated coldly.

Jessica shrugged. "I know you're cutting off your nose to spite your face," she said. "Intolerance just isn't in, Li. Here, let's ask Liz. She'll tell you."

Elizabeth and Enid had just come through the lunch line. Jessica waved at them. Elizabeth waved

91

back. Then she and Enid strolled over to Cheryl and Rosa's table and sat down.

That was no surprise, Jessica decided. Elizabeth and Lila did *not* get along; of course Elizabeth would rather sit with Cheryl. Jessica glanced back at the lunch line. "There's Maria," she observed.

Jessica and Lila watched Maria walk forward with her tray. Halfway across the cafeteria, Maria paused. She looked at Jessica and Lila, then she looked at Cheryl and the others. With an apologetic smile at Jessica, she headed to Cheryl's table.

Thirty seconds later, Sandra Bacon and Jean West approached. They faced the same choice, hesitated in the exact same way. Jessica suppressed a grin when they opted to sit with Cheryl too.

Lila's jaw dropped. "Close your mouth," Jessica advised. "This isn't the dentist's office. And don't feel bad. Here comes Amy—*she'll* sit with us."

Lunch tray in hand, Amy marched purposefully in their direction. But at the last second, she veered suddenly to the left.

Lila watched in disbelief as Amy squeezed into the last empty chair at Cheryl's table. "*What* is going on here?" she demanded.

Jessica grinned. "It's the handwriting on the wall, Li. Can't you read?"

"No, I can't," Lila said sarcastically. "Please translate it for me."

"Sweet Valley High has gotten used to the idea of an interracial romance," Jessica complied. "It's totally uncool to be a hold-out on this topic, Li."

"Oh, is it? Do you really think the final verdict is in?"

Jessica nodded. "Well, I don't agree," Lila declared with a sniff. "It's one thing for everybody to be nice to Cheryl at school, when Steven's not around. But what about the rest of the time? What about after school, the weekends, real life?" she challenged. "Correct me if I'm wrong, but I don't see people beating Cheryl's door down, inviting her and Steven to parties and stuff like that."

Lila had a point, but Jessica was not about to admit it. "Well, there weren't any parties last weekend," she rationalized.

"No, but there's going to be a big party this weekend," Lila rejoined, her eyes glinting.

Jessica had no choice but to reveal her ignorance. "There is?"

Lila nodded. "It just happens that *my* neighbor, Andrea Slade, is planning a bash at her house for this Saturday night—she told me this morning when I bumped into her on the way to school. I don't need to tell you," Lila added in a portentous tone, "that this will be the biggest party she's given since she and her dad moved to Sweet Valley."

"Wow," Jessica breathed. She remembered when she and Lila had spent a good portion of their free time spying on the old Kitterby mansion down the street from Fowler Crest, because the rock star Jamie Peters had moved in there. The first time they glimpsed Andrea, a new girl at school, hanging out by the swimming pool with Jamie, they had erroneously concluded that she was his girlfriend. It never occurred to them that their heartthrob had a teenage *daughter*.

"Of course it won't be an open party," Lila continued. "Invitation only. And only the coolest people will be there. If you don't get an invitation to this party, you're nobody."

Jessica was starting to get Lila's drift. "Is Andrea going to invite Steven and Cheryl?"

Lila smiled. "I have no idea. I got the impression from Andrea that she probably wouldn't get around to formally inviting people until later in the week—maybe after school on Friday. She really doesn't want to make a big deal out of it. But this party *is* a big deal. It seems to *me* that this is the ultimate test for Cheryl and Steven, don't you agree?"

Jessica wrinkled her forehead, trying to recall whether Andrea and Cheryl even knew each other. "Andrea's a nice girl," she mused. "She's rich, but she's not a snob like you. She's not the prejudiced type."

"I'm not prejudiced," Lila protested calmly. "Just realistic." Lila took another bite of her sandwich, then swallowed. "By the way, Jess, have you heard the latest? Rumor has it that since Andrea and Nicholas Morrow broke up, she's developed a crush on our dear friend *Bruce*, of all people!"

"How can she like *him*?" Jessica groaned.

"Bruce can be awfully charming when he wants to be. He probably already has Andrea wrapped around his little finger. Yep, I bet he'll be helping her draw up the guest list for the party," Lila speculated with obvious pleasure. "It's sure to be *very* exclusive."

Jessica recalled her and Elizabeth's recent run-in

with Bruce at the Valley Mall and resisted the urge to start chewing her fingernails. No doubt about it, in Sweet Valley High society, getting invited to a party could make a reputation—or break it. Would Cheryl and Steven and their brave new love make the final cut?

"How's this spot?" Annie asked Tony, Cheryl, and Steven as they cut across the main lawn of the town park on Friday night.

"It's halfway between the bandstand and the concession stand," Tony observed. "I'd say perfect."

Annie put down the picnic basket. Steven and Cheryl spread a blanket out on the grass. "What a night to listen to music under the stars," Cheryl said, taking a deep breath of cool, blossom-scented evening air.

Tony and Annie sat down on the blanket and put their arms around each other. Annie snuggled close to her boyfriend. "It's unbelievably romantic," she agreed.

Still standing, Cheryl shifted her feet uneasily. For some reason, Annie and Tony's frank display of affection made her feel self-conscious. *They can't keep their hands off each other. Will they think it's strange if Steven and I don't hang all over each other too?* she wondered.

Steven dropped onto the blanket. Gingerly, Cheryl settled down next to him—close, but not so close that they were touching. She wrapped her arms around her tucked-up knees, hoping her discomfort wasn't evident.

She tried to relax, to focus on something other

than Steven's nearness. It really was an incredibly beautiful evening. The sinking sun had streaked the western sky with purple and orange; tiny lanterns glimmered along the paths of the park; random bars of music wafted through the air as the orchestra members tuned their instruments.

Annie and Tony were chatting about the charity fund-raising road race he was participating in the next day. Meanwhile, a conspicuous silence had fallen between Steven and Cheryl.

"This was really a fun idea," she said. "It reminds me of summer in New York and going to concerts and plays in Central Park."

"You can't beat a free outdoor concert," Steven confirmed. "Too bad it's not rock instead of classical music, though."

"I *like* classical music," Cheryl reminded him.

"Well, just don't be surprised if I doze off on you," he kidded.

Before Cheryl could respond, the conductor lifted his arms. The concert began, a crescendo of music drowning out the sound of Cheryl's sigh.

Cheryl looked at Annie and Tony out of the corner of her eye. Annie rested her head on Tony's shoulder; Tony rubbed his cheek against her hair. They looked so happy—anyone could tell in an instant that they were totally in love. *Whereas Steven and I . . .*

Cheryl frowned, wondering. *We're not acting like a real couple. We look like two strangers who just happen to be sitting next to each other. Steven doesn't even appreciate this concert!*

The image of another boy popped unbidden into

Cheryl's head, a boy who loved all kinds of music —classical, jazz, blues. . . .

"Hey, Cheryl," Annie hissed. "Want to go with me to buy a soda?"

Cheryl snapped out of her reverie, a guilty flush heating her cheeks. "Yeah, I'm thirsty," she replied. "Want anything, Steven?"

"Sure, a lemonade, if they have it," he said.

Annie and Cheryl headed toward the concession stand, weaving among the blankets and lawn chairs. There were lots of couples, Cheryl noted— old couples, young couples with babies, middle-aged couples. She wanted to talk to them, to ask them: Do you feel right together? What makes your relationship work?

"This is fun." Annie gave Cheryl's arm a quick squeeze. "Double-dating, I mean. It seems like such a sisterly thing to do—it's the kind of thing I always imagine Jessica and Elizabeth doing."

Cheryl smiled. She held her brown arm next to Annie's fair one. "We're *not* exactly Jessica and Elizabeth!"

Annie laughed. "No. But we're sisters all the same. And I'm so happy for you and Steven, Cheryl. I really am."

"Thanks. I'm—I'm happy, too. For you and Tony."

Annie beamed, her eyes glowing like stars. "Oh, Cheryl, I wish I could explain how it feels. Tony and I had something special before—we were crazy about each other. But this time around, after breaking up for a while . . . We really know *why* we're together. We didn't just fall in love, we *chose* each other, you know?" She elbowed Cheryl. "Not that falling in love isn't great. Don't get me wrong! But this is even better." Annie grinned sheepishly. "Am I making any sense or do I just sound like a lovestruck idiot?"

A wistful smile touched Cheryl's face. "You make perfect sense," she said softly.

They returned to the blanket, each carrying two styrofoam cups of lemonade. Cheryl settled down to enjoy the concert. But it was harder than ever to surrender to the music. Her thoughts wouldn't let her.

Annie and Tony know why they're together, Cheryl reflected, *but what about Steven and me? Why are we together? Did we choose or did we fall? And where do we go from here?*

Cheryl sipped her lemonade. Maybe she and Steven wouldn't go anywhere. Maybe they would just do this over and over, every single weekend. *We sure can't count on getting invited to many parties*, Cheryl thought bitterly, thinking about the invitation she hadn't received from Andrea Slade.

So that was what it would be like from now on—Steven would drive down to Sweet Valley, or else she'd visit him at college. That was what couples did. The prospect was like a door slamming in Cheryl's face. She was outside in a big, breezy park, but suddenly she felt trapped and smothered.

Then guilt pricked her, as sharp as a needle. Cheryl turned to Steven, remembering all he had meant to her since she'd moved to Sweet Valley, how strong he had been that fateful night at the

Crooked Canyon Café. Other people might be fickle, but she could count on Steven.

Gently, Cheryl placed a hand on top of one of his, mesmerized by the contrast between her dark and his light skin. *I'm not trapped,* she told herself silently. *I'm free.* Dating Steven made her free; it made them both free. Didn't it?

Nine

"I handled the highway," Cheryl exclaimed as she parked the VW in the Wakefields' driveway late Saturday afternoon. "I'm so proud of myself!"

"There'll be no stopping you now." Steven climbed out of the passenger seat and stretched his arms over his head. "You could drive across the country. All the way to New York if you wanted!"

"I wouldn't mind doing that this weekend," Cheryl mumbled, half under her breath.

Steven walked around to Cheryl's side. "Well, Manhattan's a little far to go just for dinner," he kidded. "Where's the action in Sweet Valley tonight?"

Cheryl shot a quick glance at him, then dropped her eyes. "Oh, I don't know," she said vaguely. "There's nothing in particular going on."

Steven peered at her face. He got the impression there was something she wasn't telling him. But

Cheryl turned her face away. "C'mon," she said, taking his hand. "You said the twins were baking today. I could use a snack."

Steven decided not to pry. If Cheryl wanted to confide in him, she would do it of her own accord.

They found the twins and their boyfriends in the backyard. "Just who I was hoping to see," called Jessica. "I was setting places for you!"

"It looks like you're cooking more than cake," observed Cheryl.

"You bet," said Jessica as she scattered place-mats, napkins, and utensils around the picnic table. "I'll tell you how it got started. Sam breezes in an hour or so ago with zinc oxide all over his nose, looking like the total beach bum that he is."

Sam saluted from his post by the smoking grill. "Guilty as charged."

"Meanwhile," Jessica continued, "thanks to my cruel twin, *I* spent the whole afternoon chained to a hot stove."

"I did not chain you!" Elizabeth protested. "You *volunteered* to bake a cake for the wedding, remember?"

Jessica ignored this interjection. "Anyway, the first thing my sensitive boyfriend does is say something totally sexist like, 'This is what I like to see—women busy in the kitchen.' "

Steven guffawed. Cheryl's lips twitched as she tried not to smile. "That's awful," she commiserated.

"I thought so too," said Jessica. "I just hate it when people make sexist remarks. Or racist remarks," she added, clearly for Cheryl's benefit.

101

Good ol' subtle-as-a-freight-train Jessica! Steven thought, wincing.

"So, what did you do?" Cheryl asked.

"I told him he was as bad as Bruce Patman, and threw a dish towel at him," Jessica replied.

"Which I promptly used to wipe the chocolate frosting from her face," Sam contributed.

"It was mocha," Elizabeth recalled.

"*And* I told him that since Liz and I made dessert, he and Todd could cook dinner," Jessica concluded.

"It seemed fair," Sam acknowledged.

"So we went grocery shopping. And voilà." Todd flourished a spatula. "The salmon is done. Let's eat!"

"This salad is delicious," Cheryl raved a few minutes later.

Elizabeth twisted in her seat to press her lips against Todd's cheek. "You guys really outdid yourselves."

"I've always been somewhat handy with the grill," Todd said modestly.

"But who'd have guessed *you* could make a perfect hollandaise sauce?" Jessica teased Sam.

"It's just one of my many hidden talents," he told her.

"What are the others?"

Sam nuzzled Jessica's neck. "You'll just have to keep discovering them one by one."

Steven dug around in his salad bowl with his fork, spearing a piece of sun-dried tomato. Ordinarily, he didn't mind the way his sisters and their boyfriends goofed around. But tonight, all the bill-ing and cooing was making him edgy. *Is it because I'm with Cheryl?* Steven wondered. He and Cheryl didn't act that way in front of other people. A frown creased his forehead. Come to think of it, they didn't act like that when they were *alone*, either. *With these driving lessons, we spend enough time together in the car, the all-American make-out spot . . . how come I never have the urge to make a pass at her?*

Steven slid his chair closer to Cheryl's. He didn't want to give anyone, including Cheryl herself, the impression that he was reluctant to be openly affectionate with her.

When they had polished off the salmon and salad, Elizabeth made an announcement. "Now for the main event!"

Steven's sisters ducked into the kitchen. A minute later they reappeared, each carrying two cake plates. "Lemon cake with raspberry filling, and angel-food cake with chocolate-mint frosting," said Elizabeth, presenting her two single-layer cakes.

"And white cake with orange-buttercream frosting, and hazelnut cake with mocha frosting," added Jessica.

"Let the official tasting begin," Todd decreed.

Elizabeth handed him a knife so he could cut the cakes. Todd passed everyone a plate with four thin slices.

Cheryl admired the array on her plate. "They're almost too pretty to eat."

Steven peered at his piece of hazelnut cake. He wouldn't go *that* far. "What happened to this one?" he wondered. "Isn't it kind of . . . flat?"

"I wasn't going to say anything, but now that

you mention it, it does look sort of like it got run over by a car," Todd volunteered.

"It might not work too well as a wedding cake," Sam contributed. "You'd have to bake about twenty layers."

Jessica's lips drew into an offended pout. "I can't believe you guys. You haven't even tasted it yet!" she cried.

They all took a bite of the hazelnut cake. Steven chewed thoughtfully, then offered a verdict. "It tastes OK, but the texture's weird."

"It's rubbery," Elizabeth agreed. "Sorry, Jess."

"But I beat those eggs for *hours*," Jessica remembered. "It's supposed to be light as air!"

"That could be the problem—the eggs," Cheryl speculated. "Do you think you might have used too few eggs, or maybe too much flour?"

Jessica considered for a moment. "I might have measured the flour wrong," she admitted. "Lila called and I was trying to talk on the phone and mix the batter at the same time." Her expression brightened. "But I bet my other cake is a lot better. Try that one!"

Dutifully, they all sampled the cake with orange frosting. Steven made a face. Cheryl choked, then coughed to cover it up. "The frosting—what an unusual flavor," she managed.

Todd was more precise. "You mean, what a *gross* flavor."

"It's bitter," said Elizabeth. "Jess, when you grated the orange rind, did you use just the very outer part?"

"Well, not *exactly*." Jessica wrinkled her nose. "I took a short cut—I peeled the orange and then put the whole peel in the food processor."

Elizabeth grinned. "That explains it."

"At least there are two more cakes," Steven pointed out. "And they're bound to be edible—Liz baked them!"

Everybody laughed. Jessica looked like she didn't know whether to join in the hilarity or burst into tears. "You were right," she wailed to Elizabeth. "I'm a horrible cook!"

Sam hugged his girlfriend. "You're a great cook," he told her. "You just made a few little mistakes. That's the whole point of practicing."

"Right," Cheryl chimed in. "It's like piano. You might play a piece perfectly in a recital, but when you're trying to learn it, you always hit a lot of wrong notes. Take my word for it!"

Jessica sniffled. Then she giggled. "If cooking is like playing the piano, it looks like I should stick to 'Chopsticks.' "

"We still have a whole weekend to create the perfect wedding cake," Elizabeth reminded her.

"Never fear, Cheryl," said Todd, slipping an arm around Elizabeth. "If I know these two, and I think I do, they'll pull it off in style."

Cheryl smiled. "I don't doubt it for a minute."

Steven looked at Todd and Elizabeth, and then at Jessica and Sam. The two couples looked so relaxed, so *natural*. Elizabeth and Todd had been together for a long time now—Steven couldn't imagine them without each other. As for Jessica, she seemed to have outgrown her role as an outrageous flirt. She was settling down with Sam and had never seemed happier.

Suddenly, Steven had a sense of déjà vu. Hanging out with his sisters and their boyfriends like this reminded him of when he was dating Cara. But there was something different about tonight, even as there was something similar. He and Cara had been tight, a solid couple; they fit right in. Whereas he and Cheryl . . .

Steven polished off the piece of lemon-and-raspberry cake. *There's nothing wrong with Cheryl*, he thought. *Liz and Jess like her—she fits in just as well as Cara did*. If there was a difference, it was *within* the relationship, under the surface. The difference was inside *him*.

The realization struck Steven like a lightning bolt. He had been in love with Cara—deeply in love. And he simply couldn't pretend to himself that his feelings for Cheryl possessed anywhere near that kind of intensity.

What's holding me back? Steven wondered. It was a question he was almost afraid to try to answer.

"You guys are going, aren't you?" Jessica said to Elizabeth and Todd.

Elizabeth nodded. "We wouldn't miss it."

"Miss what?" asked Steven.

"Andrea Slade's party," said Elizabeth. "It's been the talk of the town all week."

Next to him, Steven felt Cheryl stiffen. *So that's it*, he thought, his jaw tightening. Obviously, Andrea hadn't invited Cheryl. *Well*, Steven supposed grimly, *we might as well get used to it. We're probably going to be left off a lot of guest lists.*

He took Cheryl's hand, silently communicating his support. At that exact moment, Jessica clapped her hand to her mouth. "Ohmigod, I can't believe

I forgot!" she exclaimed. "I got so spaced out over these stupid cakes. Andrea called here this afternoon, Cheryl, and she was absolutely frantic because she hadn't been able to get through to you and Annie. It turned out she was dialing the Whitmans' old phone number. *Anyway*, she made me promise to extend a special invitation to you and Steven on her behalf."

Steven and Cheryl glanced at each other, startled by this turn of events. Jessica bounced happily in her chair. "You got invited! Aren't you psyched?"

"You mean because it looks like we're about to receive the Sweet Valley High seal of social approval?" Cheryl asked somewhat dryly.

"Well, sure," said Jessica, clearly puzzled by Cheryl's lack of enthusiasm.

"I'm up for it if you are," Steven said to Cheryl. She shrugged.

"Great." Jessica beamed. "We can all go together!"

"Great," Steven echoed.

"It was the best party of the year so far," Jessica gushed to her parents on Sunday morning. "Everybody danced their feet off—Andrea has the coolest sound system."

"Of course she does," said Elizabeth. "Her dad's a rock star!"

"Jamie wasn't there." Jessica sighed. "But Cheryl actually got to sit on his piano bench and play his piano. Then we made these dance videos and showed them on a big screen. Steven and Cheryl's was the best. They were the hit of the whole party! Absolutely everyone thinks they make *the* coolest couple. Even Lila admits it now!"

Steven yawned. "Do you really think I care what Lila Fowler thinks?"

"Everyone cares what other people think," said Jessica. "Don't pretend you're any different than the rest of us, Steve-o."

Mr. Wakefield slipped a huge omelet onto a serving platter and cut it into thirds. Some English muffins popped up from the toaster and he tossed them on the platter too. "Here's your breakfast, kids."

Jessica, Steven, and Elizabeth sat down at the table. Steven and Elizabeth started eating, but Jessica was too caught up in her story to stop for food. "I think it's great that people are seeing the light," she chattered on. "I mean, it was touch and go there for a while, Steven. But you two hung in there and it was worth it!"

Mrs. Wakefield pulled up a chair. "I'm glad you and Cheryl are getting along so well," she said to Steven.

"You should see them together!" Jessica exclaimed. "They're crazy about each other. Right, Liz?"

Elizabeth paused with her English muffin raised halfway to her mouth. Crazy about each other. That might be how it looked to Jessica, but it wasn't Elizabeth's impression. Her gaze flickered to Steven's. He dropped his eyes. "Ummm," Elizabeth mumbled vaguely.

"You know, Mom and Dad, you guys hardly even *know* Cheryl," Jessica went on, twisting in her seat to look at her father. "Don't you think you should do something about that?"

"I'd be happy for a chance to get to know Cheryl better," said Mr. Wakefield.

"Then let's all go out to dinner tonight," Jessica suggested.

"That's a nice idea," Mrs. Wakefield responded. "Don't you think so, Ned?"

As he poured more beaten eggs into the skillet for the next omelet, Mr. Wakefield grinned wryly. "Any excuse not to cook!"

"I wonder where we should take Cheryl." Jessica pondered the question. "Someplace nice—we want her to know how happy we are that she's going out with Steven. I know! How about Villa Marino?"

Elizabeth glanced at her brother. He looked distinctly unenthusiastic about the entire prospect. "Isn't that kind of fancy?" Elizabeth said. "I mean, maybe Steven and Cheryl don't want us to make such a fuss over—"

"It's our *duty* to make a fuss," Jessica reminded her twin, adding under her breath, "Do you want Cheryl to think that Mom and Dad are like the parents in that old movie, *Guess Who's Coming to Dinner?* That they don't want to have anything to do with her?"

"Of course not," Elizabeth answered.

"Then shut up!" Jessica advised succinctly.

Once again, Jessica had the last word. "Then it's settled," Mr. Wakefield said heartily. "Villa Marino it is."

Steven cracked a stiff smile. "I'd better phone

Cheryl and tell her what's on the itinerary. Who'd have predicted we'd end up being such a popular couple?"

Mrs. Wakefield opened her menu and smiled at Cheryl. "So, are the wedding plans all set?"

Cheryl nodded. "We've hired a caterer and decided on a menu, booked musicians, ordered flowers, and sent out invitations. The only thing we still need to take care of is the photographer." She laughed. "I guess my dad doesn't trust anyone else to use a camera correctly!"

Steven tugged at his tie, loosening it slightly and resisting the temptation to tear it off altogether. Elizabeth had been right; this place was too fancy. Apparently, he was the only one who was uncomfortable, though. His parents were chatting animatedly with Cheryl; the twins pored over their menus, debating the virtues of various pasta sauces. Steven recalled Jessica's remark to Elizabeth that morning, the one she hadn't intended for him to overhear. This wasn't at all like *Guess Who's Coming to Dinner?* His parents had taken Cheryl into their hearts without a moment's hesitation.

Mom and Dad support us, Steven thought. *In fact, everybody accepts us these days.* What a change from a couple of weeks ago! He felt like the scene at the Crooked Canyon Café had taken place in another lifetime. This meal, this gesture on the part of his family, more than made up for it. He and Cheryl had come full circle.

Steven looked across the table at Cheryl. She smiled at him, nudging his foot with hers under the table. In the dim light of the restaurant, her eyes glowed like stars in a velvety dark sky.

Steven blinked. For a split second, Cheryl's face had blurred and he imagined another pair of warm brown eyes gazing into his . . . Cara's. Now Cheryl was officially his girlfriend. She had taken Cara's place in his life—his entire family seemed to take that for granted.

How did it happen so fast? Steven wondered. One minute he and Cheryl were just good friends. The next they were dating, Sweet Valley's hottest item. He supposed one thing just led to another. And another, and another . . .

Suddenly, Steven thought about where dating had almost led him and Cara not that long ago: to the altar! A cold fist closed around his heart, choking him. He stared at Cheryl, envisioning her in a wedding dress like the one she was describing to his mother, the one Mrs. Whitman would wear the following weekend. First you dated, then you got engaged and you were talking about the rest of your life. Was that really what he wanted with Cheryl, a long-term relationship, maybe even *marriage* someday?

Steven stuffed a piece of Italian bread in his mouth. *Geez, don't get in such a state*, he berated himself. It didn't have to go *that* far between them. The problem was, though, Steven recognized, he didn't want it to go *anywhere*.

He had to face it. Even though Cheryl was a great girl, if he could go back in time and stop this relationship from ever starting, he would do it in a second. After all, he had never even thought of

111

Cheryl in a romantic way until that night at the beach. . . .

Steven traveled back in his mind to that emotionally charged scene. *Why did I look at her in a new way?* he asked himself. *Why did I kiss her?* Had he felt sorry for her because of what happened at the restaurant? Or was it more like taking a dare?

Steven remembered the antagonism they had encountered earlier that evening. *I was embarrassed at first, but then I was angry. I just reacted.* Reacted—the word resounded in Steven's brain. Looking at it that way, did the kiss on the beach have anything to do with Cheryl at all?

Suddenly, Steven was filled with doubt. He tried hard to relive that moment when he had looked down into Cheryl's tragic, tear-stained face. Had he seen her right then as a *person*, or just a *black* person? When it came right down to it, was he really any better than those punks in the leather jackets?

It was as if someone had held a mirror up to his face, and Steven didn't like what he saw. He couldn't bring himself to meet Cheryl's eyes, to meet anyone's eyes. Cheryl's beauty, his family's tolerance, all good things in the world were like a slap in the face. Remorse and guilt stole away Steven's appetite; the crust of Italian bread slipped from his fingers. What was he going to do now?

Ten

I'm breaking all the driving rules I taught Cheryl, Steven thought wryly as he raced south. Passing on the right, speeding up instead of slowing down at yellow lights ... He'd better hope there weren't any state troopers on the road!

Steven braked the VW, moderating his pace somewhat. What was the rush, anyway? It wasn't like he was looking forward to the conversation he intended to have with Cheryl.

He had been back on campus for three days, and for three days he had thought about nothing but Cheryl and the painful self-revelations of the previous weekend. Just that morning, during a political-science lecture, he had decided he couldn't keep his feelings bottled up any longer. If he waited until the weekend to see Cheryl, he ran into the problem of the wedding. What was he going to do, take Cheryl aside while her father and Mrs. Whitman exchanged vows of everlasting love, and tell her he wanted to break up with her?

Steven squinted into the sun. *Relationships are so weird,* he reflected, not for the first time in his life. They got started so easily sometimes; you called a girl up, you danced with someone at a party. But they were always, *always* hard to end.

I could turn around and drive back to school.... Steven fought off the temptation. He and Cheryl really needed to talk. It was going to hurt, but he had to be honest with her.

Once again, Steven sorted through his jumbled emotions, reviewing the short but explosive history of his friendship and romance with Cheryl Thomas. When they had first met, when they were just friends, they had a great time together, Steven reflected. He didn't think about racial stuff. Their color difference wasn't an issue for either of them. Not until the night they stopped at the Crooked Canyon Café, the night at the beach when they had gotten caught up in the heat of the moment and shared a kiss.

It could have—should have—ended there, Steven knew. But it hadn't. He had pretended to be attracted to her, pretended he wanted a relationship with her. And that was when he did Cheryl an injustice. For the first time he had made something out of their racial difference. Unknowingly, he had lied to Cheryl and to himself and to the whole world.

I want our old feeling back, Steven thought with a rush of nostalgia. A genuine friendship was worth far more than a false romance. That is, if they could still *be* friends, after this.

Steven exited the highway and headed for Calico Drive. As he turned onto the street, he hoped his sisters weren't home from school yet; he would prefer they didn't know about this particular visit. He pulled into Cheryl's driveway. Now he found himself hoping *she* wouldn't be home. She might not be—he hadn't phoned ahead to tell her he was coming.

But Cheryl opened the door immediately. "Steven! What are you doing here? Cutting class?"

"I had only one class today—it was over at noon," Steven explained. "I guess I just had an urge to go for a drive." He cleared his throat. "And to see you."

Cheryl ducked her head. Did she suspect something? Steven couldn't tell. "Well, come on in," she said brightly. "I was just heading out back to do some homework, but I'd much rather talk to you."

A minute later, they were sitting next to each other in deck chairs. There was no backing down now. Steven took a deep breath. "Actually, this isn't totally spontaneous," he confessed. "I need to talk to you about something, and I didn't want to do it over the phone."

Cheryl raised her eyebrows. "What is it, Steven?"

He leaned forward, taking her hands in his. "Cheryl, I've been thinking about us and—"

"Cheryl! Steven!" someone hollered.

Steven knew that voice. He looked over his shoulder, exasperated. *Great timing, as always!*

Jessica bounded across the lawn toward them. "What are *you* doing here?" she demanded of Steven.

115

"Well, I—"

Not waiting for Steven to finish, Jessica whirled on Cheryl. "Cheryl, you're really the one I want to talk to. You have to help me and Liz decide. We're going with the basic golden wedding cake, but what kind of filling do you think your parents would prefer, raspberry or chocolate-mint?" Jessica paused, but only long enough to take a breath. "And how many guests will there be? We need to know so we can figure out how many tiers the cake should have." She put a hand on her hip. "Then there's the *aesthetic* question. Should we decorate the cake with fresh flowers, or flowers made of buttercream frosting delicately tinted with food coloring?"

Cheryl burst out laughing. Steven couldn't help grinning.

Jessica frowned. "What's so funny? This is important, you guys!"

"I know." Cheryl assumed an appropriately straight face. "And I really appreciate all the trouble you're going to with this cake, Jessica. Let's see . . . I think raspberry filling would be best. Raspberries are Mona's favorite fruit. And fresh flowers would be pretty—I can ask the florist to put some aside for you. As for the guest list, we're expecting about sixty people." She smiled. "But maybe you should bake an extra layer—I bet everybody will want seconds."

"You're absolutely *sure* you want raspberry and not chocolate-mint," Jessica asked, double-checking.

"Absolutely."

"OK." Jessica spun on her heel and took off

again. "Thanks. See ya!" she called over her shoulder.

Steven rolled his eyes. "She's nuts, in case you hadn't noticed."

"She's taking this *very* seriously," observed Cheryl.

"Well, you're probably safe with raspberry filling. Raspberries don't have pits!"

Cheryl laughed. Then she tipped her head to one side, her eyes questioning. "What were you about to say, Steven?"

Steven rubbed his jaw. He'd completely lost his concentration when Jessica dashed off; it was as if she had taken his brain with her. "Uh, I was about to say that—"

"There you are, Cheryl. Oh, hi, Steven!"

Steven turned. This time it was Annie. She waved at them from the kitchen window. "Don't forget we have an appointment at the Designer Shop in twenty minutes," she called to Cheryl.

"Oh, right. Just let me get my purse," Cheryl replied. "I'll meet you at the car." She got to her feet. "We're having our bridesmaids' dresses altered," she explained to Steven. "If I'd known you were coming over . . ."

"It's OK."

"I'll tell you what. Walter and Mona are out of town on a shoot, and Annie and Tony are going out later. Why don't we make dinner together?"

"I'll drop by around six," said Steven.

"Good." Cheryl looked up at him for a moment. Then she stood on her tiptoes and brushed his lips with hers. "See you later."

117

"So long."

Steven watched Cheryl disappear into the house. Then he cut across the lawn to his own backyard, trying not to feel too relieved. He wasn't off the hook completely—he would get another chance to talk to her tonight. And that was what he wanted, right?

He lifted a hand to his mouth, still feeling Cheryl's butterfly-soft good-bye kiss. She was on her way to try on her bridesmaid dress . . . the wedding was in just three days. All eyes in town were on Mr. Thomas and Mrs. Whitman—and on him and Cheryl. Steven frowned, his resolution disintegrating. Wouldn't breaking up with her now send the wrong message? After all they had been through together, could he really do this to her?

Rosa, whom Cheryl and Annie had picked up on their way to the mall, squeezed into a dressing room at the Designer Shop with Cheryl. "What a beautiful dress!" she exclaimed.

Cheryl held the bridesmaid dress against her body and faced the mirror. The tea-length dress had cap sleeves and a sweetheart neckline, all in a soft floral print of dusty blues, pinks, and greens. "It is pretty," Cheryl agreed. "We were lucky to find something that Annie and I both liked."

"Try it on," Rosa urged.

Cheryl pulled off her cotton sweater and stepped out of her denim skirt. Removing the dress from its hanger, she drew it carefully on over her head.

Rosa zipped her up. "It's a perfect fit," she raved. "You're gorgeous, Cheryl."

Cheryl stared at her reflection. She didn't *feel* gorgeous. Cowardly and ugly was more like it.

It was really time to take action—Steven was driving down to visit on weekdays now. She couldn't keep leading him on, letting him believe she felt more for him than she actually did. But just now, she had let a perfect opportunity slip through her fingers. Jessica and Annie had provided her with a convenient excuse not to confront Steven, and she had taken it.

Cheryl pivoted, examining the back view of the dress. *But what would I have said? That I'm interested in another boy? That whenever I kiss Steven, I imagine I'm kissing Martin Bell instead?* Was that really what was going on? Cheryl wasn't one hundred percent certain. But it was the only explanation she had been able to come up with for the vague sense of guilt that was oppressing her.

Rosa met Cheryl's eyes in the mirror. "Is something wrong, Cheryl? Don't you like the dress?"

Cheryl realized she was frowning. She made an effort to relax the muscles of her face, but she couldn't quite manage a smile. "No, the dress is fine." Cheryl heaved a deep sigh. "I know I should be in a great mood these days, Rosa. But for some reason ..." She searched for a word that could sum it up. None seemed quite adequate. "Anxious."

"About what? About the wedding? Or is there a problem between you and Steven?"

Cheryl didn't know where to begin. Her feelings about Steven and about the wedding were so complicated, and for some reason they were all tangled up together. "I just want everything to be perfect

119

on Saturday," she burst out. "You know, all the details. My toast," she added, biting her lip.

"Well, things don't have to be *perfect*," Rosa reasoned. "I mean, sure, flowers and food and music and toasts and stuff are important. You want things to look nice and you want people to have a good time. But you shouldn't *worry*. The most important part of the wedding is already taken care of."

Cheryl's forehead wrinkled. "What's that?"

Rosa smiled. "Your dad and Mrs. Whitman, silly! Their love for each other. That's what the wedding's all about, right? Can anything else really matter much, in comparison?"

Dad and Mona . . . that's what it's all about. "No," Cheryl agreed at last, though she was still troubled. "Nothing else really matters."

Steven wandered down to the kitchen. "Jess traded her apron for a bikini, huh?" he observed, straddling a chair.

Elizabeth looked up from the mixing bowl she was washing out at the sink. "I got stuck with the dishes," she confirmed.

"Some things never change!"

Elizabeth laughed. "I can't get mad at her, though. She always has such a good excuse! Today she just *had* to get outside because, and I quote, 'Showing up at the wedding with a good tan is just as important as showing up with a good cake.'"

Steven grinned. "What a con artist."

Elizabeth dried her hands on a dish towel. "So," she said conversationally. "Jessica said you buzzed down from school to see Cheryl." She didn't want to be nosy, but she couldn't help wondering why, if that was the case, her brother was hanging out alone at home.

Steven shrugged. "That was basically the reason. Cheryl had to go to the bridal shop with Annie."

"Oh. She must be getting pretty excited about the wedding, huh?"

"I suppose."

Elizabeth leaned her elbows on the table. For weeks now, she had had the feeling that Steven's new relationship wasn't working out quite the way he had hoped. Not that he'd *said* anything to that effect; he didn't talk about it. *Maybe he's ready to talk now, though.*

"A wedding is really an emotional event," she remarked, taking a roundabout approach because she knew Steven would only get defensive if she asked flat-out about his problems with Cheryl. "Everybody's happy, but things can also be tense. I bet Mrs. Whitman and Annie are nervous wrecks. Cheryl's probably too sensible to get stressed out, though."

"Oh, I don't know about that." Steven raked a hand through his hair. "She's a *little* stressed. Actually, *I'm* a little stressed," he admitted.

"You two have been under a lot of pressure. It's not easy being pioneers!"

Steven laughed grimly. "You don't know the half of it!"

Elizabeth tilted her head to one side. "What do you mean?"

Steven studied his sister's face, clearly debating

121

whether or not to confide in her. "A couple of weeks ago," he said after a moment, "the first time Cheryl and I went on a date . . . Actually, it was before our first *date* date. Things were still just platonic between us. Anyway, we went for a drive and we stopped at this little hamburger place."

As he talked, Steven's hands clenched into fists. "We walked into the restaurant," he continued, "and everybody stared. If it had just been a couple dirty looks . . . But it was more than that. There were some punks, guys about my age. They said some nasty things, and they said them loud enough for Cheryl and me and probably everyone else in the restaurant to hear."

Steven lifted his gaze to Elizabeth's. The naked pain she saw in his eyes tore at her heart. "Liz, I'd never experienced anything like that," he said, his voice hoarse. "Maybe we've lived sheltered lives, you and me and Jess. Maybe we were just incredibly lucky to be raised by such tolerant, loving parents. I can't tell you how that scene got to me. I wanted to kill those guys!"

"I bet you did," Elizabeth whispered.

"But violence isn't the answer, you know?" Steven shook his head vehemently. "It would have been stupid to pick a fight. It wouldn't have fixed anything. A few more black eyes aren't going to make the world a better place."

"That's a tall order, making the world a better place," Elizabeth said quietly.

"I know. But we have to start somewhere."

Do you love Cheryl, though? Is this relationship more than just a crusade? The questions jumped to Elizabeth's lips, but she bit them back. They were too personal.

"About Cheryl . . . You'll do what's right, Steven," she said instead. "If you trust your own good judgment and listen to your heart."

"Listen to my heart—that sounds easy enough. Lately, though, I think my heart's been speaking a foreign language."

Elizabeth smiled. "Well, hey, doesn't Cheryl have a flair for languages? Maybe she can help you with a translation."

Steven's lips curved, but the smile didn't reach his eyes. "I don't know. Neither of us seems to be too good with words these days. You should see the hard time we've been having composing a toast for her to give at the wedding!"

"I get a writer's block when I don't really know what I'm trying to say," Elizabeth reflected.

A shadow flickered across Steven's eyes. He didn't speak; he didn't need to. Elizabeth knew what he was thinking. To listen to your heart, to express your heart, you had to *know* your heart. That was the whole problem.

"Homemade pizza dough." Cheryl showed Steven the pan. "We can put anything we want on top. I've got tomato sauce, green peppers, red peppers, mushrooms, onion, garlic, mozzarella—"

"All of the above," said Steven.

Cheryl grinned. "The works, huh?"

"What could be better?"

Standing side by side at the kitchen counter, they chopped vegetables and sprinkled them over the

123

sauce-topped crust, finishing with handfuls of grated cheese. Cheryl popped the pan into the oven.

"It'll take about twenty minutes," she told Steven. Opening the refrigerator, she took out two cans of soda. "Want to sit outside?"

"We'll be running the risk of having Jessica barge over," Steven warned.

"Let's live dangerously."

They sat down on the deck, in the exact same position they had been in that afternoon. Cheryl knew they were both thinking of the interrupted conversation. "Did you want to talk about something?" she asked Steven, hoping he wasn't going to make some kind of declaration of undying love. "I got the feeling before that you didn't just drive down on a whim."

"I did, though." Steven pushed a dark shock of hair back from his forehead. "All I was going to say before was that ... I like being with you, Cheryl."

Cheryl smiled softly. "I like being with you too."

"And I'm looking forward to Saturday, to the wedding."

"I wouldn't want anyone else by my side," she told him.

Steven's dark eyes held hers. "Honestly?"

"Honestly." A powerful wave of emotion washed over her. She had meant what she said, every word. She *did* like being with Steven, she did want him by her side. *So what's wrong? Why am I dissatisfied?*

"Are you nervous about giving your toast?" Steven asked, popping the top on his soda can.

"The toast—don't remind me." Cheryl sighed. "I'm not nervous, I'm just not *ready*."

"You mean you're revising it again?"

Cheryl gave him a thin smile. "I'm starting *over* again." Jumping to her feet, she retrieved the notebook she had been scribbling in before Steven arrived. "Let's get it right this time, OK?"

"OK." Steven threw back his head, contemplating the pale blue evening sky. "It *should* be simple. You just want to say something about how you feel on the occasion of your father joining in marriage with Mrs. Whitman."

"Right." Cheryl uncapped her pen. "I feel . . . I feel proud." She wrote the word in big block letters. "In their position, a lot of people wouldn't have stayed together or even gotten together in the first place. But Dad and Mona went for it. They forced the world to accept them on their own terms."

"It had to be tough, though," Steven reflected. "There must have been times when they wanted to call it off, when they weren't sure it was worth it."

"Of course," Cheryl agreed, writing fast. "Love is never easy, especially the kind of love they have. But they stuck it out."

"They're proof that an interracial romance can work," Steven asserted. "They're rising above prejudice."

"And they're taking us all with them." Cheryl scrawled a few more lines in the notebook. "By getting married, Dad and Mona show us *all* how we can be better people."

"That's it." Steven lifted his hands. "There's your toast!"

Cheryl looked down at what she'd written. Key words jumped off the page at her. Pride ... proof ... prejudice ... difficulty ... uncertainty ...

Her hands tightened on the notebook. "What's the matter?" Steven asked.

"Where's the joy, the celebration?" Cheryl cried. "Why can't I get at it? Why doesn't it come through?"

"Let me see." Steven read over her shoulder. "Hmm. Well ... Look, we've been at this for weeks. I just don't see where we can make it any better. It's fine."

Cheryl fought back tears of unhappiness and frustration. She shoved the notebook aside. "Time's running out. This'll have to do."

Steven put a hand on her arm. "It'll be all right," he murmured gently.

Cheryl knew he was just trying to make her feel better, but his words and his touch were anything but comforting. The toast wasn't right, she recognized in despair. It would never be right.

Eleven

Cheryl inched her stool closer to the kitchen counter. Taking a gold-edged paper card from a pile, she checked the alphabetized guest list and applied her calligraphy pen. *Elizabeth Wakefield*, Cheryl wrote in elegant script. She set the finished place tag aside so the ink could dry and took another blank tag. *Jessica Wakefield*, she wrote next. And then, *Steven Wakefield*.

Cheryl stared at the place tag. Steven Wakefield . . . Shouldn't that name send chills down her spine whenever she saw it or spoke it? Instead, Cheryl felt the familiar vague pang of guilt and dissatisfaction. *I wouldn't feel this way if I were really in love with Steven*, she thought, dropping the calligraphy pen and resting her chin on her hand. *I love him as a friend, but I'm not in love with him. I never was.*

At this point, that much was clear in her mind. So why hadn't she been able to bring herself to break off their romance? Why did it seem so impossible to go back to the way they were before that one Sunday night?

"Cheryl, it's dark in here!" Mona Whitman flicked the light switch. "Isn't that better?"

"Yeah." Cheryl glanced at the window. "I guess the sun kind of set on me."

Mrs. Whitman joined Cheryl at the counter and examined the place tags. "Those look nice." She shook her head, smiling. "I can't believe that this time tomorrow . . . !"

"You'll be my dad's wife."

"And your stepmom."

"I'm glad," Cheryl said sincerely.

"Me too."

Mona paced over to the refrigerator. "Want some fruit salad?" she asked. "Or should we open this carton of fudge-swirl ice cream?"

Cheryl laughed. "Mona, I can't believe you're pigging out, tonight of all nights!"

Mona spooned into the ice cream, smiling. "It must be prewedding jitters."

"You're nervous?"

Mona handed Cheryl a spoon and sat down on a stool. "A little. But in a good way. Your father and I are about to take a very big step."

"You really are." Cheryl traced Steven's name on the tag with her finger. "I've never told you this, Mona, but I understand what you're doing and I think it's great."

"What do you mean?" Mrs. Whitman asked, puzzled.

"You know, dating and now marrying my dad.

I think it's great that you two don't care what people think, that you decided to show everyone. I'm proud of you and Dad for proving that there shouldn't be a barrier between the races."

Mona raised her eyebrows. "We're not out to prove a point, Cheryl. Where would you get an idea like that? This marriage is about love, like any other marriage. It isn't about showing anything to anyone."

"You mean, it's about love between blacks and whites," Cheryl persisted. "Between a black man and a white woman."

"No." Mrs. Whitman shook her head emphatically. "You've got it all wrong. Marriage is the expression of love for a particular person, not a group of people. I love your father because of who he is—I love Walter Thomas, the man. It has *nothing* to do with the color of his skin." Mona's tone was gentle but firm. "Any more than it has to do with how much money he makes or how tall he is, or anything superficial like that."

Cheryl flushed. "So, you're saying I'm superficial," she said defensively.

"I wasn't talking about you, honey. I thought we were talking about me!" Mrs. Whitman looked down at the place tag with Steven's name on it. Then she studied Cheryl's face intently. "In my opinion, it would be wrong to marry or even date a person just to make a statement, even a positive statement," she said quietly. "It shouldn't be about what Steven Wakefield represents, Cheryl. It should be about who Steven Wakefield *is*."

Cheryl turned away from Mona, too confused

129

and angry to respond. For a long moment Mona didn't speak or move either. Then Cheryl felt a light kiss on the top of her head. Mona's sandals clattered across the kitchen floor and into the hall.

Silence settled over the room. All at once, Cheryl felt alone, abandoned, scared. She wanted to call after Mona. She wanted to feel strong, loving arms around her; she wanted someone to hold her. *Just like that night at the beach*, Cheryl thought, *after the Crooked Canyon Café . . .*

She and Steven had needed to hug, to kiss. Cheryl's eyes stung with tears. They had come together, briefly, for the right reason. But they had *stayed* together for the wrong one.

"Um, this is yummy," Jessica pronounced, licking the knife.

"Jessica!" Elizabeth grabbed the knife and rinsed it off at the sink. "If you eat all the frosting, we won't have enough to cover the cake."

"OK, OK, don't have a breakdown." Jessica lifted the largest layer pan and gently inverted it onto a round glass cake plate. "The bottom tier," she pronounced proudly. "Isn't it beautiful?"

"It's perfect," Elizabeth agreed, admiring the golden cake. "No air bubbles and no burned parts."

Jessica grinned. Her hair was dusted with flour and she had a smudge of raspberry filling across one cheek. "And I measured everything twice!"

Carefully, Elizabeth sliced the layer in half horizontally so they could spread it with raspberry filling. They did the same for all four layers.

"I can't wait for everybody to see our cake," Jessica said when they had assembled the tiers.

Elizabeth handed her a knife. They began smoothing on the buttercream frosting. "I just hope they're hungry. It's a small wedding and this is a *huge* cake. There's probably enough here for everyone to have three or four pieces!"

Jessica used her knife to create a basket-weave pattern in the frosting. "When *I* get married, I'm inviting everyone I know," she told Elizabeth. "I want hundreds of people and a big band so we can dance all night."

Elizabeth laughed. "Who's the lucky groom?"

"Sam, I guess. He'd look cute in a tuxedo, don't you think?"

"And that's the most important criterion," Elizabeth teased.

"Of course not!" Jessica dimpled. "He's also a fantastic dancer."

"So, it'll be a total blowout, with Sam dancing around in a tux. What are *you* going to wear?"

Jessica pondered this crucial question. "I just can't see myself in an enormous princess-type wedding dress with tons of satin and lace," she said at last. "How about a white leather mini?"

Elizabeth rolled her eyes. "But with a floor-length veil, right?"

Jessica grinned. "What a fashion statement, eh?"

Elizabeth turned the cake so they could frost the other side. "So?" Jessica prompted.

"So what?"

"So, what about *your* wedding? What is it going to be like?"

131

"Oh ..." Elizabeth blushed slightly. "I never think about that sort of thing."

"Yeah, right." Jessica snorted. "And the sun orbits the earth instead of the other way around. You *know* you've been fantasizing about marrying Todd ever since you guys went on your first date."

Elizabeth couldn't entirely deny it. Whenever she thought about the future—where she'd go to college, her career, having a family of her own someday—Todd was usually part of the picture. A big part.

"All right," she capitulated. "*If* I were going to get married, and *if* I were marrying Todd, I think we'd have a small wedding."

"Boring," Jessica pronounced with an exaggerated yawn.

"You'd be my maid of honor," Elizabeth continued.

"Well, that part's OK."

"And Enid and Penny and Olivia would be my other bridesmaids. You'd wear long pink dresses—"

"Blue dresses," Jessica corrected. "It's a much better color on me."

"Cornflower-blue," Elizabeth suggested. Jessica nodded approval. "And I'd wear ... Mom's wedding dress. We're the same size—it should fit."

"Oh, Liz." Jessica's eyes grew misty. "You'll be such a beautiful bride!"

Elizabeth laughed. "Don't cry on the cake," she warned.

Sniffling, Jessica reached for a paper towel. "Who would Todd pick for groomsmen?"

"His dad could be his best man, and maybe he'd ask Ken and Aaron and Winston to be ushers," Elizabeth replied. "Oh, and Steven—I bet he'd ask Steven."

"Steven," Jessica mused. "I wonder what *his* wedding will be like."

"I don't know. I just hope it's not across the state line in Nevada with a justice of the peace officiating!"

"Do you think he'll marry Cheryl?" Jessica asked.

Elizabeth tried unsuccessfully to picture her brother and Cheryl exchanging wedding vows and rings. She couldn't—not after the conversation she had had with him the other day. "No," she said at last. "I don't think he will."

"Cheryl would make a cool sister-in-law, though," Jessica argued.

"But that's not the issue," Elizabeth reminded her. "If Steven and Cheryl aren't happy together . . ."

"Who says they aren't?"

Elizabeth didn't want to violate Steven's confidence, so she just shrugged. "I guess it's too soon to tell," she said diplomatically.

"Yeah, it's too soon for all of us," Jessica agreed. "Sam and I won't be ready to get married for five or ten years at least."

"The good thing is, we have all the equipment." With a wicked smile, Elizabeth lifted up one of the cake pans. "Now that we know how, it'll be a breeze baking the cake for *your* wedding. How many guests did you say you're inviting?"

"Get that thing away from me," Jessica declared.

"I'm ordering *my* wedding cake from a bakery, no two ways about it!"

Cheryl crossed her bedroom in the dark and sat down at her desk, facing the window. The night breeze blew back the curtain; the yard was bathed in moonlight.

The white, beribboned tent was already set up on the lawn next to the deck, where the luncheon would be served. On the opposite side of the yard, an arch of flowers had been constructed; Walter and Mona would exchange their vows beneath it the very next morning.

Cheryl gazed upon the scene. Then she blinked. Her eyes were blurred with tears—was she seeing things?

No—there were two shadowy figures in the yard. They stepped into a pool of moonlight. Cheryl saw that it was Annie and Tony.

Hand in hand, the pair walked across the grass and stood beneath the flowery trellis. Tony wrapped his arms around Annie; she lifted her face to his for a kiss.

Cheryl's heart contracted painfully. *I'll never feel for Steven what Annie feels for Tony*, she realized, sighing deeply. *Never.*

But that was OK. Pulling a tissue from the box, she wiped her eyes. If it turned out that she and Steven were meant to be friends and nothing more, that wasn't necessarily a bad thing, or even a sad thing. The sparks just weren't there. And Cheryl finally understood that it was a function of personality, of chemistry—or rather the lack of it—not of race.

She reached for the spiral notebook on the corner of her desk and opened it to the page where two days ago she and Steven had scribbled the most recent version of her wedding toast. Tearing the sheet from the notebook, she crumpled it into a ball and tossed it at the wastebasket.

She lifted her eyes to the window again. Annie and Tony were gone; the yard was empty. *A clean slate*, Cheryl thought.

She sat up a little straighter, feeling light, as if a burden had been lifted from her shoulders. Taking a deep, steady breath, she smoothed her hand over a fresh sheet of paper. Then she picked up her pen and began to write.

Twelve

Cheryl slipped the comb one last time through Annie's hair. "There," she said. "You're all done."

They both looked into the bathroom mirror. Annie turned her head from side to side, admiring the few sprigs of baby's breath that Cheryl had woven into her hair. "Do you like it?" Cheryl asked.

Annie nodded. "It looks very ... bridal. Oh, Cheryl!" Her eyes sparkled with excitement. "Isn't this fun?"

Cheryl smiled. "It really is. C'mon, let's go see how your mom's doing."

The two girls hurried down the hall to Mrs. Whitman's bedroom. They found Mona just slipping her arms into the sleeves of her tea-length ivory silk dress. "Just in time," Mrs. Whitman announced. "Will you zip me up, honey?"

Annie zipped the dress and then gave her mother

136

a cautious hug. Cheryl heard them both sniffle; her own eyes brimmed with sentimental tears.

"Oh, Mom," Annie whispered. "You're a vision. I don't think there's ever been a more beautiful bride. Walter's just going to fall over when he sees you."

Mrs. Whitman laughed. "I hope not!" Taking something from the top of her dresser, she turned to Cheryl. "You can give me a hand too, Cheryl. You did such a nice job with Annie's hair. Will you put on my veil?"

The short veil made of delicate netting was attached to a hair comb. Cheryl pulled back Mona's hair on both sides of her face, leaving some to cascade down her back. Twisting the hair into a knot, she secured it with the comb.

Mrs. Whitman dropped a kiss on her cheek. "Thanks, honey."

Cheryl returned the kiss. "Thank *you*," she whispered. "For our talk last night."

Mrs. Whitman smiled. "That's what moms are for." Then she clasped her hands together. "So, girls. I guess I'm ready!"

"Are you sure?" Annie fretted. "Do you have on something old and something new, something borrowed and something blue?"

"Oh, no," Mrs. Whitman moaned. "Do I have to go through that routine the second time around?"

Annie nodded firmly. "It's good luck, Mom."

"Well, the dress is new." Mona laughed. "And I'm old."

"No, you're not," Annie protested. "That wouldn't count, anyway."

"These are old, then." Mona put her hands to her pearl earrings. "They were a sweet-sixteen present from my grandparents."

"How about something blue?" asked Annie.

Mona considered, then shook her head. "No, I'm not wearing anything blue. Or anything borrowed, for that matter."

"I know," Cheryl said suddenly. "Wait here."

She darted down the hall to her own bedroom. Pulling open a dresser drawer, she riffled through a pile of lingerie until she found what she was looking for: a small square of white linen, stitched in blue with the script letter *M*.

"A handkerchief," Mona said when Cheryl presented it to her. "And it has my initial. It's lovely!"

"It was my mother's," Cheryl explained. "Her initial was *M* too. I'd—I'd like you to have it."

"If you gave it to me, it wouldn't be something borrowed as well as something blue," Mrs. Whitman pointed out. "I'll carry it with me today. But it's a very special keepsake, Cheryl. You shouldn't part with it."

She tucked the handkerchief into her beaded clutch. Then she smiled at Annie and Cheryl. "Now I'm *really* ready."

"But you have to stay up here until Walter goes downstairs," Annie cautioned. "He's not supposed to see you before the ceremony."

"Well, then, why don't you go hurry him along, Cheryl?" Mona suggested. "And here, take this." She handed Cheryl a florist's box containing a white rosebud boutonniere. "Tell him it's from me, with love."

Cheryl smiled. "I'll tell him."

She found her father downstairs, pacing in front of the den window and watching the guests troop down the driveway and disappear around the side of the house. "Did we set up enough folding chairs?" Mr. Thomas worried. He pointed to a small white cloud in the distance. "Do you think it's going to rain?"

"We have plenty of chairs, and it's not going to rain," Cheryl assured him.

"How's Mona doing?"

"Great. She sent you this, along with her love." Stepping up to her father, Cheryl pinned the rose to his lapel. "The finishing touch."

"How do I look?"

Cheryl beamed up at him through her tears. "Incredibly handsome, Dad."

Mr. Thomas wrapped his arms around his daughter. "Now, don't start bawling," he teased.

"I can't help it. I'm just so happy for you and Mona." Cheryl whispered, overcome with emotion. "I'm happy for all of us."

"We're going to make a wonderful family," Mr. Thomas agreed.

"A wonderful family," Cheryl echoed. She took her father's hand. "C'mon, Dad. You don't want to keep Mona waiting!"

"It's a masterpiece," Jessica declared. "If I may say so myself."

The caterer had positioned their cake at the far end of the white-draped buffet table. Elizabeth placed one last pink blossom alongside it and sighed. "It's really too pretty to eat."

Jessica disagreed. "I didn't have time to eat breakfast and I'm *starved*. I may just eat a whole tier by myself." Turning her back on the cake, she lifted a hand to shield her eyes from the sun and scanned the crowd milling about the Thomases' and Whitmans' backyard. "C'mon, let's find Sam and Todd. I want to get a good seat!"

They came across Todd and Sam tossing a Frisbee with Tony and Steven in the side yard. "You clown, you're going to get all sweaty in your nice suit!" Jessica lectured Sam.

Sam stopped in his tracks, his eyes lighting up with admiration at the sight of the twins. "Wow, look at you two," he raved. "I don't know, this may be against the rules. Isn't the bride supposed to be the most beautiful woman at the wedding?"

Elizabeth had borrowed an outfit from Enid—a pale yellow silk dress—and in her hair she wore a lace bow. Jessica, however, had splurged on a peacock-blue minidress with big black buttons all down the front. Now she struck a pose, pivoting so Sam could enjoy the view from every angle. "Do you really like it? It was kind of an impulse purchase."

Sam pulled her to him for a hug. "You look smashing."

"Sam said it for both of us," Todd told Elizabeth, squeezing her hand. "You're the prettiest girl here."

Elizabeth stood on tiptoes to kiss him. "And you're the handsomest guy," she murmured.

"I saved seats for us," Tony said. "In the second row of chairs, right behind the relatives." The very next instant, they heard the first lively notes of a trumpet fanfare. "Let's get over there!"

Elizabeth and Jessica hurried across the lawn as fast as their high heels would permit them. It was almost magical, Elizabeth thought as she slipped into a folding chair, how an ordinary backyard could be so transformed! The festive white tent shimmered in the sun; everywhere there were bouquets of silver balloons and bunches of wildflowers tied with big white bows: the music of the trumpet lifted all hearts far above the concerns of every day.

Elizabeth stared at Mr. Thomas, who was standing in front of the arch of flowers flanked by his two groomsmen. *What must he be feeling right now?* she wondered.

At that moment, an excited murmur rippled through the crowd. There was a dramatic pause and then the trumpet processional began.

Annie, her usually pale cheeks bright pink with nervous excitement, was the first to walk down the aisle. "Look at her," Tony said in a low voice, nearly bursting with love and pride.

"What a pretty dress," Elizabeth whispered to Jessica.

"She's holding that bouquet so tightly, her knuckles are white!" replied Jessica.

Cheryl followed Annie at a slow, graceful pace, her chin held high. "Now, *she* doesn't look nervous at all," Elizabeth observed to Todd this time.

Cheryl caught Elizabeth's eye and smiled. Elizabeth and Jessica both waved excitedly. "That looks like so much fun," Jessica hissed. "I hope to get to be a bridesmaid someday!"

"I bet you'll get to be one a bunch of times," her twin assured her.

Now a hush fell over the wedding guests. The moment they were all waiting for had finally arrived. Elizabeth held her breath.

She wasn't the only one. There was a collective sigh when Mona Whitman appeared. Annie's mother was always striking, but Elizabeth was sure she'd never looked more beautiful than she did today.

Mona started down the aisle, her eyes fixed on the man who waited for her at the other end. At the sight of her, Walter Thomas's broad shoulders straightened and his eyes lit up like stars. The expression of perfect happiness on his face brought a lump to Elizabeth's throat.

Mona and Walter joined hands under the arch of flowers. Mirroring the gesture, Todd took Elizabeth's hand and pressed it warmly. She turned, gazing up at him with shining eyes. "I love you, Liz," Todd said, very softly so no one else could hear.

"I love you too," she whispered.

With a contented sigh, Elizabeth looked back at Mona and Walter, soon to be husband and wife. She rested her head against Todd's shoulder, wondering. *Someday, will Todd and I stand together at the altar? Who knows?*

"I promise, Walter, to love and cherish you, in sickness and in health, through good times and hard times, for as long as we both shall live."

Steven and the others watched as Mrs. Whitman bent her head and slipped the gold wedding band onto Walter's finger. Then the minister took both Mona's and Walter's hands in his. "With these rings and vows, you have pledged yourselves to a lifelong partnership," he declared, beaming. "May peace, joy, and fulfillment be the result of this union. It gives me great pleasure to pronounce you husband and wife!"

Mr. Thomas and Mrs. Whitman shared an exuberant kiss. Cheers broke out in the crowd. Steven grinned.

"They did it!" Todd exclaimed, hugging Elizabeth.

"Oh, I'm going to cry," Jessica wailed. "Liz, do you have a tissue?"

As the trumpet soared into a joyful recessional, Walter and Mona strolled up the aisle, arm in arm. In their wake came Annie and Cheryl, on the arms of Walter's groomsmen. Steven stood, gazing intently at Cheryl. She looked unbelievably beautiful in her flowered dress, with fresh flowers in her hands and in her hair. Everything was so beautiful, so romantic, so inspiring. . . .

Cheryl sought out Steven with her eyes and flashed him a happy smile. He smiled back, doing his best to ignore the hollow feeling in his heart.

After the bridal party had passed, the rest of the guests poured out onto the lawn. "I can't wait till it's my turn at the buffet table," Jessica confided to Steven, hungrily eyeing a waitress with a tray of hors d'oeuvres. "I'm jealous of you sitting at the head table with Cheryl—you get to eat first!"

Steven chuckled. "I'll see if I can slip you a few tidbits to tide you over."

Leaving his sisters and their boyfriends, Steven approached the throng around the bridal party. He could barely glimpse Cheryl; every few seconds, someone else pressed forward to congratulate her with a hug or a kiss.

Just as he managed to make his way to her side, the photographer whisked Cheryl and her family off for a photo session. "I'll meet you over at our table," Cheryl called to Steven over her shoulder.

He lifted a hand, acknowledging the plan with a wave. Then he wandered back toward the tent. Everywhere he looked, people were talking and laughing, hugging and kissing. *What a happy day*, he thought, feeling somehow outside of it all.

A waiter held a tray in front of Steven. He chose a hot shrimp-and-artichoke square and walked on, mulling over the ceremony he had just witnessed. *To love and to cherish, in sickness and in health, through good times and hard times, for as long as we both shall live. . . .* The words Mona and Walter had spoken were simple and pure. Steven winced, remembering the toast he and Cheryl had put together on Wednesday. It had seemed tolerable to him then, but today, in the context of the newly married couple's vows, Steven had a sinking feeling that it was going to sound jarringly inappropriate.

He shoved the thought from his head. The toast was the least of his worries; there was still the whole problem of his relationship with Cheryl to resolve.

Locating his seat at the head table, Steven waited with Tony for the bridal party to arrive. Finally, Cheryl and Annie ran up, still clutching their bouquets.

"Wasn't that wonderful?" Annie cried, throwing her arms around Tony.

Cheryl embraced Steven, with somewhat more restraint. "The caterer told me we should head up to the buffet and start things rolling," she told him. "Are you ready?"

He grinned. "I'd be happy to set a good example by filling my plate to the absolute limit."

After all the guests made their way through the buffet line and sat down, Mr. Thomas's best man, Jonathan, rose to his feet, a glass of champagne in his hand. "I'll make this brief, because I know the two girls have something to say," Jonathan promised. "I'd just like you all to raise a glass with me to toast my good friend Walter, his lovely wife Mona, and their delightful daughters. May the sun always shine on this family as brightly as it is shining today."

Steven lifted his glass. "Are you nervous?" he asked Cheryl.

She shook her head, a strangely serene expression in her clear brown eyes. "Not at all."

Annie stood up next, her hand trembling as she held her glass aloft. "Um . . ." She glanced at the notecard on which she had printed out her toast in tiny handwriting. "I'd like to share with you my thoughts on this happy occasion. When I first learned I was getting a new stepfather . . ."

Annie's toast was a touching reflection on what

it meant to be a family. The tone was just right—funny, hopeful. She got a few laughs, but by the time she finished, there were also quite a few people blowing their noses.

As Annie sat down, Steven felt like applauding. The toast had suited her, and it suited the occasion. His palms suddenly grew damp with anxiety. *How are people going to respond to Cheryl's speech?* he wondered.

He was about to find out—it was Cheryl's turn. Steven saw her take a folded sheet of paper out of her purse. Unfolding it, she scanned it quickly. Then she turned the page down on the table and rose to her feet.

Cheryl looked down at Steven, and then across the table at her father and stepmother. "Something precious and wonderful has brought us all together today," she began, her voice high and clear. "Love."

Something precious and wonderful? Love? This wasn't the toast he and Cheryl had been working on for weeks. She must have revised it again.

As Cheryl continued, Steven realized she hadn't just *revised* the toast. She had rewritten it completely.

"What makes this love special is what makes all love special," Cheryl said. "My father and Mona found each other. In this whole big scary world, they found each other. I know that Mona makes my dad's life complete, and he does the same for her. I can't imagine them without each other, and I guess that's what marriage is all about." Cheryl smiled at Mona, who was blotting her eyes with a

146

tissue. "I feel incredibly lucky that I'm going to have this example of deep, true love right before me every day."

Suddenly, Steven understood. Cheryl's toast addressed her parents and their new marriage, but through it she was also speaking to him. And her message was as clear as a beam of light. *All that racial stuff we were getting at—it was totally off base,* he realized. *Real love doesn't have anything to do with political ideas or public stances. It has to be private and freely reached, otherwise it isn't actually love at all.*

Cheryl finished her toast. All around the tent, people raised their glasses. Steven lifted his as well. "Cheers," he said in a voice that was husky with emotion.

Cheryl sat back down next to him. Steven put out a hand and touched her shoulder lightly. She turned toward him, and for a long moment they just gazed into each other's eyes. Cheryl didn't need to speak; her toast had broken through with the truth that for weeks they had both slowly struggled to recognize. And Steven knew he didn't need to say anything either. Cheryl could read his understanding, and his acceptance, in his eyes.

She smiled tremulously. Steven wrapped his arms around her and hugged her close. "You're a great friend," Cheryl whispered.

"You too," said Steven.

Suddenly, the tent was ringing with voices and laughter and the clatter of china and silverware. The wedding luncheon got under way.

Cheryl and Steven drew apart, laughing. Jonathan's wife, Belinda, smiled at them from across the table. "So, when are you two lovebirds getting married?" she teased.

Steven put his arm around Cheryl's shoulders and smiled. "In spite of the fact that we make a *very* attractive couple, we're just friends," he told Belinda.

"The *best* of friends," Cheryl added.

Thirteen

"You've got to be kidding." It was late Sunday morning and Lila had invited Jessica to play tennis at the country club so that she could get the scoop on the Whitman-Thomas wedding. Jessica had dropped her bombshell, and now Lila almost dropped her tennis racket. "They *broke up*?"

With her left hand, Jessica tossed a bright new tennis ball in the air. With her right, she swung her racket in a smooth, powerful arc, smashing the ball across the net. "Yep."

The serve was an ace; Lila didn't even try to return it. "When?" she demanded. "Where? Why?"

"I don't know too many details," Jessica confessed. She pulled another ball from the pocket of her tennis skirt. "All I know is that one minute, Steven and Cheryl were a totally devoted couple, and the next thing they were telling everyone at the wedding reception yesterday that they were just friends."

"I don't get it," Lila grunted, this time returning Jessica's serve with a slicing cross-court backhand. "They go out of their way to thumb their noses at social convention and they get away with it—they become the latest thing. And then, just when all the fuss settles down, they break up!"

"Maybe they just wanted to prove a point," Jessica guessed, although she really didn't have the first idea what had motivated her brother and Cheryl.

"And what point would that be?"

"That people should be friends with and date anybody they want to." Jessica smashed the ball at Lila. "That it's only sticks-in-the-mud like you and Bruce Patman who make judgments according to how big a house someone lives in, or which club they belong to, or the color of their skin, or what have you."

"Ha." Lila returned the shot. "I wouldn't give them that much credit. I think they just blew it, like every other dumb couple that ends up on the rocks."

"I can't believe how cynical you are."

"I'm realistic," Lila corrected. "Face it, Jessica. I *am* right about most *things*."

"Name one thing you've been right about recently!" Jessica challenged, delivering her most deadly overhead smash.

Lila tapped the ball so that it just barely cleared the net and dropped into Jessica's court. "I said I was going to whip you in straight sets, and I'm doing it."

Jessica dove forward, her arm stretched full length. She lobbed the ball to the baseline. It was still in play. "In your dreams, Li," she gasped. "In your dreams!"

"Guess what? I passed!" Cheryl shouted to Steven.

Steven jogged down the steps from his dorm and around the front of Mr. Thomas's Buick. Grabbing Cheryl, he swung her around in a dizzy, triumphant circle. "Congratulations!"

"Yep, I'm a licensed driver," Cheryl confirmed proudly. "I drove here straight from the Motor Vehicles Department and I didn't make a single mistake."

"You must not have made any mistakes during the driver's test, either."

"Well . . ." Her eyes crinkled. "I scored one hundred percent on the written test. But I almost failed the parallel-parking part of the road test. I just *froze*! It took me five tries to back into the space, and even then I was still a mile away from the curb."

"*You*, park a mile from the curb?" Steven kidded.

She punched him lightly in the arm. "Hey, I've come a long way. Want to take a spin so I can show you?"

"How 'bout taking a walk instead?" he suggested. "It's a gorgeous day. C'mon, I'll treat you to a soda."

They stepped into the dormitory lobby so Steven could flick some coins into the drink machine. Carrying icy cans of soda, they started off across the green, grassy quadrangle. Cheryl glanced at Steven out of the corner of her eye. He looked rumpled and relaxed, totally at ease with himself, and with her. *Just like old times,* Cheryl thought, her heart light and happy.

"Thanks for coming up," Steven said. "I mean, on a Wednesday and all."

"I had to celebrate with *someone,* and you were the natural choice. I'd still be riding the bus if it wasn't for all those driving lessons!"

Steven raised his soda can. "Here's to parallel parking."

Cheryl imitated the gesture, smiling. "And the automatic transmission on Dad's Buick!"

They reached the south end of the quad where the lawn sloped down to a row of athletic fields. They sat down side by side on a wooden bench at the top of the hill. "It's really good to see you," Steven said, slinging an arm companionably around her shoulders. "But I'm sure glad we're not still dating!"

Cheryl burst out laughing. "Me, too. Do you think there's ever been a weirder breakup?"

Steven shook his head. "Nope."

She remembered their moment of truth during the wedding-day luncheon. "It was pretty painless, in the end."

"It just took us a while to figure out that we'd started something we didn't want to finish."

"I knew something wasn't right," Cheryl admitted. "I was on the verge of breaking up with you a couple of times—"

"Hey, me too!"

"But I never went through with it. I kept thinking I had some kind of responsibility. Like, our duty as a couple was to set a great example to the rest of the world."

"I was afraid of hurting you," Steven confessed. "That night, at the restaurant, those jerks with the shaved heads . . ." His jaw clenched. "They made me so mad, but I also felt powerless. I felt like the only thing I could do was let you know that I was different from those other white guys."

"All I could think about was Dad and Mona," said Cheryl. "What they were up against, and how I never wanted them to have an experience like that."

"And then there was the infamous toast." They both laughed.

"Now that's where I *should* have been thinking about Dad and Mona, but I was really stuck thinking about us," Cheryl concluded.

"I guess we both felt we had to prove something," said Steven. "To prove that it's OK for people of different races to hang out together and care for each other."

"And it *is* OK." Cheryl turned dark, serious eyes to Steven. "It was always OK."

Steven smiled crookedly. "So, should I apologize for kissing you that night at the beach?"

"Naw. It was a great kiss!" They both laughed. "I don't think that was our mistake," Cheryl continued. "We had good reasons for wanting to be close that night. We wanted to defy everything those punks at the café stood for—we wanted to stand for something better."

"It just wasn't a healthy basis for a relationship," Steven concluded. "Our mistake was staying together in order to prove a point."

"And because of social pressure," added Cheryl. "I was so caught up in what everyone at Sweet Valley High thought about it!"

For a minute, they sat in friendly silence, gazing out at the green playing fields. Suddenly, Cheryl had a thought that made her burst out laughing. "You know, Steven, in one way, it's too bad we're not going out anymore."

"How come?"

Her eyes twinkled mischievously. "Dad and Mona are off on their honeymoon—Annie and I have the house all to ourselves."

"Don't tempt me!" he kidded.

"Hey, Wakefield!" someone shouted from the bottom of the hill.

Steven shaded his eyes. "What's up, Bob?"

"A soccer game. We need someone to play wing."

Steven looked at Cheryl. She nodded. "I really should head back," she said.

"Be right there," Steven called to Bob.

He and Cheryl stood up. "So, you probably won't be coming down to Sweet Valley this weekend," she remarked.

"Not this weekend," Steven said. "You won't need me around so much, now that you've got your license. Maybe the weekend after."

"Whenever."

"Call and tell me the latest gossip, OK?"

Cheryl smiled. "Will do."

Steven started down the hill to join the soccer game. "So long," he called back to her.

She waved. "See ya!"

Cheryl headed back across the quad to where she'd parked the car. She didn't feel sad thinking that she wouldn't see Steven for a few weeks; she felt free. *A whole weekend to myself . . . hmm*, Cheryl mused. *What am I going to do with it?* The possibilities seemed endless.

She was so busy daydreaming, she almost walked right into somebody. She looked up just in time—and right into a familiar face. "Martin!" she exclaimed, her eyes brightening.

"Hey, Cheryl!" Martin grinned. "Nice to see you. What's new?"

"Oh, nothing much. I just dropped by to tell Steven I got my driver's license."

"Are you sticking around for dinner?" Martin asked.

"No, I have homework, and Steven probably does too."

"What a studious couple," Martin kidded.

Now's as good a time as any to get the message across! Cheryl decided. "Studious maybe, but we're not really a *couple*," she told Martin. "We're just good friends."

This was news to Martin—he raised his eyebrows in surprise. But he didn't comment, or ask questions.

"Well," Cheryl said after a moment. "See you around."

"See you around," he echoed.

As Cheryl continued on toward the Buick, she

stifled a small sigh of disappointment. Then, suddenly, she felt a hand on her arm and someone spoke her name.

She turned. Martin smiled at her shyly. "Uh, would it be all right—could I call you sometime?"

Cheryl smiled back at him. "I'd like that," she said. "I'd like that a lot."

After the next Sweet Valley High prom, life will never be the same . . .

Elizabeth and Jessica Wakefield have been planning a jungle-theme prom for weeks, but what should be a night of romance and fun turns into a tragic nightmare.

Experience love, death, loyalty, and betrayal in one horrifying tale, starting with Sweet Valley High's newest Magna Edition, **A NIGHT TO REMEMBER**.

Following this chilling seven-book mini-series:
Sweet Valley High #95, **THE MORNING AFTER**
Sweet Valley High #96, **THE ARREST**
Sweet Valley High #97, **THE VERDICT**
Sweet Valley High #98, **THE WEDDING**
Sweet Valley High #99, **BEWARE THE BABY-SITTER**
and the final terrifying conclusion in Sweet Valley High #100 . . .